Riverside

Miguel Antonio Ortiz

Irene Weinberger Books
an imprint of Hamilton Stone Editions
Maplewood, New Jersey

Cover Design by Adalberto Ortiz

Library of Congress Cataloging-in-Publication Data

Ortiz, Miguel Antonio.
  Riverside / by Miguel Antonio Ortiz.
    pages ; cm
  ISBN 978-0-9836668-8-2 (acid-free paper)
  1. Families--Fiction. 2. Single men--Fiction. 3. Mate
selection--Fiction. 4. Interpersonal relations--Fiction. I. Title.
  PS3615.R825R58 2015
  813'.6--dc23
                              2015000158

Chapter 1

I WAS ACQUAINTED with Sharon Hobart for only a short time. I never did figure her out, but when I heard about her death, something inside of me snapped.

I had been sitting at my desk for a few hours, and I was itching to get up and stretch my legs. Stock market quotes kept ticking across my brain and interfering with the story I was trying to write. Data Terminal had shot up much faster than I expected, and Continental Containers had announced a merger. I stood to make another bundle. In the past two years I had quite multiplied my assets. I told myself that being on top of the market was something I owed my heirs, but deep down I knew I was just trying to take the easy way out.

Temptation was always sitting on my shoulder when I was up against a blank screen. I figured a two-hour struggle entitled me to a rest. I decided to go down to the corner and pick up the paper. I rode the elevator down sixteen floors. In the lobby, I tried to avoid being detained by Maximo Contreras, the doorman. He had been a boxer, but he had retired early from the ring. Now, he was content to look mean and keep any potential malefactor away from the Fifth Avenue address where I lived along with sundry other folk, some of whom you wouldn't care to meet.

Max was somewhat taller than I, so when talking to him, I tilted my head up to keep my eyes on his lips. Not that I was deaf and into lip reading. I had gotten into the habit of focusing on his face to make him feel important.

He liked to talk about boxing, or anything else that came to mind, a born talker, not the usual trait of a fighter, or so I

thought until I met Max. He had a round bulgy face with a
lump here and there, injuries acquired in the ring no doubt.
He wore a gray uniform that implied some military quality
in a doorman. An inveterate gambler, ever since he found
out that I played the market, he had been trying to figure a
way of getting a piece of the action. He was convinced that
I was privy to all sorts of inside information.

"It's just like playing the horses," I once said to him.
"It's all luck."

"I know it's like playing the horses, and that's how come
I know it ain't got nothing to do with luck," he said.

Anyway, I had trouble walking away from anyone trying
to tell me anything, and Max was on to that. I knew every
fight of his career blow for blow. But just then, I wasn't in
the mood for any of his long anecdotes.

"Some headline this morning," he said.

"I'm in a hurry. I'll catch you later," I said and rushed
out before he could pin me down.

Having managed to get by Max without the usual
conversation, I headed west towards Sixth Avenue,
wondering what in the paper that morning was so interesting
to him. If anything unusual had been happening in the
market, my broker would have called. Then I remembered
that I had turned off the phones to keep any ringing from
interfering with my creativity, and I had neglected to check
for calls before I stepped out. Feeling a September nip in the
air, I proceeded down Waverly.

When George, the newsstand guy, a rotund little man
whose hairless top glistened in the sun, saw me approaching,
he pulled out the *Wall Street Journal* and the *Times* and
handed them to me as soon as I got there.

"You don't want a copy of the *Post* too, do you?" he
asked.

I looked down at the stack of papers. The *Post* headline

read: "Nude Actress Dead at EVRT," under it a picture of Sharon. The story read: "Sharon Hobart, an up-and-coming actress, was found dead at the East Village Repertory Theater. Her nude body was discovered at the bottom of an air shaft. The victim had been bound and gagged, and apparently hurled down from the roof. A police spokesperson stated that they yet have no suspects, but that a vigorous investigation is underway." The story went on, but I couldn't read any more. All I could think of was Sharon's body hitting the ground.

In a daze, I walked down Greenwich Avenue to Gabriel's Pub. Don't think that it was named after the angel; it wasn't. It was named after Garcia Marquez. *One Hundred Years of Solitude* was the owner's favorite book, so I once asked Sam why didn't he just call the bar One Hundred Years. He said he didn't want to associate it with the solitude. I suppose he had a point there. I ordered a double scotch straight up.

"What's the matter Marc? You look like you just received another rejection slip," Sam said, as he handed me the drink.

"Something like that," I replied.

Photographs of published patrons hung on the walls. Sam was well up on my stagnant writing career, but he never met Sharon. I had not taken her there, because Gabriel's was my place to hang out with other writers. It was that sort of place. She wasn't part of that. I kept that separate. Maybe if I had a book published and my picture hung on the wall, I would have brought her over to look at it. Maybe that had been one of my dreams, one no longer possible.

"I guess one never gets used to rejection slips," he said.

"No," I said, "never."

"Still, you have enough experience not to take it so hard."

"You would think so, wouldn't you," I said.

Chapter 2

I HAD MET SHARON at Frannie Thompson's. That should have been warning enough, but I didn't heed the prompting of my better nature. Maybe that's my fatal flaw. I don't always listen to that little voice saying, "Walk away. You're going to get creamed, if you don't."

Frannie was a friend from way back. She had an unerring sense of where money and power resided, and she gravitated in that direction. I often wondered whether she really liked me. She convinced me that she wasn't interested in me as a lover. We were strolling in Central Park one day when she told me about another guy.

"I'm madly in love," she said.

I felt a slight pang like when the dentist inserts the needle into the gum. It's just that slight sensation, and I know that nothing else is going to hurt me.

"Are you?" I asked trying to stay calm.

"I am," she said. "He's a wonderful guy. I know you're going to like him."

I knew right off that I wasn't. I knew it the minute she said he was a wonderful guy in a tone of voice that implied that it meant a great deal to her that I think so too. I only saw him once. Oliver Schwan, tall, blond, and imperious, an expert on the Far East, he consulted for corporations, for the State Department, for think tanks. He was connected to some university or other. I wasn't too attentive to those details. When I met him, I noticed the lines beginning to form around his eyes although he was young. His family had oodles of money, but money didn't mean anything to him. It was like the air he breathed. I would have liked to cut off his supply (of money) and watch him suffocate. It was disturbing, not to say disgusting, to watch Frannie relate to him. She stuck to him like nettle. He remained oblivious of her most of the time. Once in a while, he condescended to smile down at her, and she opened up like a morning glory at dawn.

I couldn't stand to see Frannie make an ass of herself. I knew he would mistreat her, and I didn't want to stick around to see it. I stopped calling her. She stopped calling me. Even after they broke up, a long time passed before we reestablished communication, and then it was too late to pick up where we had left off. And anyway, neither one of us knew exactly where that was.

Frannie decided to live out on the West Coast for a while. During that time we scarcely communicated, but when she returned, with manic intensity she went about trying to reestablish old connections. We renewed our friendship. At first, I thought it natural. Everybody gets lonely. Everybody needs other people. "No man is an island..." and all that stuff. But Frannie seemed never satisfied. When you were with her, she seemed to drink you up, consume you. You were always aware that you were being spiritually devoured, but somehow you made no effort to escape. You came back again and again. Frannie despite all this gorging was never satiated. When she was through with you for the moment, she dropped you, as if you no longer existed, and moved on to the next person. Throughout, she had the power to keep you from being so offended that you lost the desire to offer yourself again.

As I said, on her return from out west, we again became bosom buddies, but after a while she stopped returning my calls. I was pissed. I decided she was no longer my friend. There were plenty of other women out there. I didn't need her. That resolution of course didn't keep me from accepting an invitation to a party she was throwing to celebrate her reemergence in New York—that was the ostensible reason. The true reason was more understandable. She wanted to show off her new beau. That was all right with me. I was anxious to meet the gentleman. I spent some time, not a great deal mind you, but some, wondering what manner of man he was. I figured for sure that he was ambitious and had money, but everything else about him was open to speculation. I didn't go to the festivity expecting to have a good time, and I didn't. I knew the kind of people who always preyed on Frannie, and I felt sorry for her sometimes. But she had made her bed. I went to the party only expecting to have an interesting time, and I did.

I took a taxi up to 116th Street and Riverside Drive where Frannie's mother, Bella Thompson, lived in one of those sprawling fifteen room apartments that most of us only glimpse in trashy novels and TV movies. The doorman gave me the once over. He was new on the job; I had never seen him before. I looked him straight in the eye and said "Thompsons." He seemed to wither a little. He was the kind of doorman that liked to give strangers a hard time, whether they were in a three-piece suit or worn-out overalls. The elevator was paneled in mahogany, and it smelled like it had recently been saturated with Lemon Pledge. I was careful not to lean on the wood; otherwise my jacket might pick up the smell for the evening.

At the door of the apartment, a stranger who seemed to be the official greeter welcomed me. I was ready to extend my hand and say, "You must be Larry." But he anticipated me. "You'll find Larry somewhere in the crowd back there," he said, cocking his head in the appropriate direction. He had a smirk on his chubby face, as if he enjoyed being mistaken for Larry. So, he wasn't Larry. I was disappointed. He was pretty much what I expected Larry to look like: slightly overfed and jovially aggressive. Anyway, he was one of Larry's henchmen. I knew the type. I moved into the throng looking for a friendly face, or at least a familiar one. No luck until I spotted Mrs. Thompson.

"Oh, there you are, Marco. So glad you're here." She said as she got up to greet me, and leaning close to my ear whispered, "I do need to talk to you."

I figured that she probably just wanted to swap recipes. She knew I liked to cook. She put her hand on my arm and squeezed it. I leaned over and kissed her on her right temple. I thought of my mother whom I hadn't seen in a few months. I made a mental note to go down to visit her as soon as I got a chance, but it wasn't as simple as it used to be now that she had moved to Florida.

In the meantime, I let Mrs. Thompson play surrogate, or perhaps it would be more accurate to say that she enticed me to do that. I had grown attached to her. She was a lady disposed to suffer with elegance. On observing her fussing with the details of decorating a room—worrying whether on a table a vase was half and inch too far to the right or to the left, or having arranged a flower display for the twelfth time and still not satisfied—one would have thought her so occupied with life's trivia as not to be able to reflect on the more profound aspect of the whole. That was but a surface manifestation of her character, a means of facing a world that she perceived as hostile and unpredictable, a world best handled through incantation. Her obsession with detail was her attempt to appease the gods—the magic by which she staved off personal disaster.

She had a profound sense of failure, and she believed that at some early point in her life she had been betrayed into an essential error from which she would never be able to extricate the remnants of her life. Her children were less than a joy to her; she feared failing to do well by them. I'm not suggesting that Mrs. Thompson had a morose personality. She was generally occupied with so many things as to lack the time to be introspective. Indeed, only through indirection did I occasionally glimpse her true concerns.

I didn't then know, nor am I sure now, what about me had at first caught the Thompson imagination. They treated me as if I were a messenger from another world, and sometimes as if I had the secret to their individual and personal salvations.

"You're a unique young man," Mrs. Thompson said to me once. "You know that?"

I didn't.

"You have more influence over Frannie than anyone else," she said. "I hope you use it well. She needs a little reining in, but I can't do it, and heaven knows Henry can't."

I was at a loss to discover how my supposed influence over Frannie manifested itself. I kept quiet.

"It would be a great load off my mind if I could see Frannie settled down. Some sort of responsibility would give her ballast. I'm sure you know what I mean." She looked at me as if we were in on some secret of human existence only parceled out to the elect. "Not that I would want to push her into anything, you understand. That's not the way to do things. I know from bitter experience."

I nodded my head. Bitter experience was written all over her face. I began to see that everything wasn't what it appeared to be with the Thompsons. They all liked to be mysterious and somewhat murky, but I got used to them.

Presently hearing that she wanted to have a serious conversation with me, I blandly smiled and said, "Sure, the night is young."

"Have you said hello to Larry?" she queried. "Oh, where is he?"

I looked around, as if that were helpful.

"Oh, there he is. Let me introduce you," she said, grabbing my hand and pulling me toward a cluster of people who were discussing the relative merit of investing in foreign currency.

Larry's look surprised me. He was less than what I had imagined, lanky, high cheekbones, hollow eyes—a sepulchral sort of fellow. I had thought Frannie partial to the meaty type. Moreover, he was older than I expected.

"Hi," he said. His eyes made an attempt to sparkle. "I've heard quite a bit about you."

"Oh?" I never know how to respond to that.

"All good," he added quickly. His lips parted in a flitting smile.

"Well, you have the advantage on me," I said, unaware, at that moment, in how many ways that was true. I wondered what Frannie was really up to.

"I hope we can remedy that," he said.

He sounded sincere, and that baffled me, or rather, somewhat annoyed me. Frannie must have reassured him that I wasn't a rival. Did he feel especially secure about Frannie, or did he automatically feel that way about everything? I wished he weren't so genial; I wanted an excuse to dislike him. He didn't provide one—other than he had Frannie.

The arrival of more guests demanded his attention, and I found myself standing alone. I made my way to the bar. Somehow standing alone with a drink in one's hand doesn't look as silly as standing alone empty handed. Everywhere I looked, little clusters of people engaged in the most animated and seemingly interesting discussions. I wandered towards the nearest group, but my presence was ignored. I retreated to another nearby cluster, but that circle also refused to receive me. This wasn't an easy crowd—not the kind that lets you in. This was the kind that made you fight your way in. Exclusion was their way of life, how they defined themselves. The habit was ingrained in their everyday lives. They behaved that way with each other. Damn them! Still, these were Frannie's friends.

I had yet to see Frannie. I looked around the room. She had to be somewhere. I made my way into the next room, and I stood at the doorway scanning for her.

"You lose your wife?" a voice purred next to me. A blond looked up at me through a pair of oversize glasses. Her black silk dress looked frictionless, for ease of undressing, no doubt.

"Yes," I replied, "but not here."

"Well, then you're looking for her in the wrong place."

"What makes you think I'm looking for her?"

"You're looking for someone."

"Am I?"

"You have that starved look."

I was definitely beginning to feel uncomfortable.

"You're in danger here," she said.

"You don't say."

"I do. You wear your heart on your sleeve. That's not done here. You're not one of them," she said looking around the room.

"One might say the same about you," I replied.

"Looks are deceiving," she claimed.

"I believe it."

"How did you get to be a corporate kingpin?"

"Is that what I am?"

"Aren't you?"

"You have all the answers."

"Every other man here is or wants to be. Why not you?"

"I thought I wasn't one of them."

"Not at heart, but men do lose their way."

"In the jungle, so to speak."

"Yes," she said. She was standing close to me now.

14

Every time she breathed in her breast rubbed against my jacket. "Are you with Allied Chemicals?"

"I wouldn't exactly put it that way," I said.

"How would you put it?"

"I own a few shares," I said. I really didn't want to get into all that, but something about her loosened my tongue.

"Oh, it's worse than I thought," she exclaimed drawing back. "You really are one of Larry's boys."

"I never laid eyes on Larry before today," I protested with more force than necessary.

"You're a stockholder," she accused.

"It's a public company," I said by way of an explanation. In quick succession, I was angry and amused that I was explaining my financial dealings to a complete stranger.

"You mean you don't work for the company?"

"I don't work for anyone but myself."

"So, you're a freelancer?"

"I suppose you can say that."

"What do you freelance at? You're not an accountant, are you? No, of course not, they're the boring type." At this point, she seemed uneasy, as if she had gone too far.

"I'm a writer," I said.

"A copywriter, like for advertising and public relations?"

"No," I said, "I'm just a writer."

She looked at me in the most puzzling manner.

"Fiction, I write fiction."

"Oh, like you write best sellers and the like."

I moved my head in the affirmative.

"Well, what's your name? Maybe I read one of your books."

There was no way out short of lying. I was going to have to confess that I was a failure as a writer. I wasn't ashamed of that. Some of the greatest writers were unappreciated by their contemporaries. I just didn't want to explain my life.

The explanation always sounded silly, and I was tired of hearing it.

At that moment, Frannie appeared to rescue me, her sense of timing fantastic. I would be eternally grateful, more or less. She made her entrance like a diva, dressed for the part in a low cut blue dress of stunning simplicity. She was the dress. Her short black hair framed her round face, from which dark eyes, accentuated by carefully groomed eyebrows, seemed to want to scorch whatever they looked at. She threw herself at me in a fit of enthusiasm characteristic of the Thompsons. One never knew whether they were feigning. But at that point I didn't care. Her perfume overpowered me, her body supple and yielding against mine. I had to admit, physically we were a right fit.

"Marc, how nice to see you," she whispered, breaking the embrace. She stood back to let me take in her entire radiant look. I don't know how she did it—how she managed to produce that glow that always made her the focal point of any gathering. "I see you already met Sharon."

"How do you do, Sharon," I said.

"Marco is one of my dearest friends," Frannie cooed, as if she really meant it.

"I can see that," Sharon said.

"Really, he is."

"What's the rest of your name, Marco?"

"Navarro," I said.

"Never heard of you," Sharon said, "but then I'm not much of a reader."

Frannie looked puzzled, but she quickly recovered. She maneuvered me away from Sharon.

"You have to be careful, Marco. I won't always be around to protect you," Frannie said when we were a safe distance from Sharon.

"She looks harmless enough."

"You're so naive," she said with so much conviction that I almost believed her. "I've been thinking about your mother, how is she doing?" she asked out of the blue.

"Basking in the sun, I suppose. I do have to go down to see her sometime soon."

"I should go also," Frannie said, perhaps to rattle me.

I wasn't quite sure whether she had noticed my mother's reservations about her. They had met while I was still married, and Frannie was introduced as my wife's close friend, true at the time.

"That would be a good idea," I said, marveling at the words coming out of my mouth disguised as veracity when I suspected that my mother would be less than pleased to see her. She had never said anything negative about Frannie, but then she rarely said anything negative about anyone. I often wondered how I had acquired my propensity to see the less favorable side of people. For certain, I had not acquired the trait, or the habit, from my mother.

"I think I can get her to like me," Frannie said.

"What makes you think she doesn't?" I asked, continuing to let my tongue waggle.

"I just have that feeling," she said.

"It's all in your imagination."

"Well, maybe you're right. I should just go visit her sometime."

"She'll be happy to see you," I said while reassuring myself that it was only talk. Certainly, Frannie wouldn't go out her way to see my mother without a self-serving reason, and I couldn't imagine her having one at the moment.

Frannie left almost as magically as she had appeared, and I found myself conversing with a young man whose jacket smelled of Lemon Pledge. I said a few words to him about the elevator, but he pretended not to know what I was talking about. A woman joined us. She worked for the State

Department and was soon to be off to some godforsaken country where we Americans were trying to save the ungrateful natives from themselves. It was such a difficult task, and she couldn't understand why the heroic benevolence of our country was so distasteful to its recipients, especially when she was an agent of its distribution. I couldn't think of any witty comments that would enlighten her, so I commiserated with her. She was very grateful and in return showed a little interest by asking me, "What are you in, Mr. Navarro?" a very interesting question with many answers. "I am in my blue socks and Calvin Klein shorts," I thought of saying, but I didn't think she would appreciate that, not in our first conversation.

On the other hand, I didn't want to make the same mistake twice at the same function. I wasn't going to tell her I was a writer. "I'm a speculator," I said thinking that there was some truth to that. The story of Bernard Baruch being thrown out of J. Pierpont Morgan's office for comparing investing to gambling came to mind, but I felt safe at the Thompsons; no one there could possibly have anything against gambling. One could, after all, invest like a gambler or gamble like an investor. All of which was beside the point, because Mrs. State Department didn't care whether I was a gambler or not. She barely managed to be polite.

"Ah," she exclaimed, "and what do you speculate in."

We were back to where we started. "In" must have been her favorite word.

"Oh, whatever," I said, "if it can be bought and sold, I buy and sell it."

"That's most interesting," she said. "You're a real businessman."

I took that as a compliment.

"My grandfather was a businessman. I admired him tremendously. Everyone did," she informed me.

I assured her that businessmen were an admirable lot. I thought she was satisfied with that, but she added, "Of course some men are not cut out for business."

"I suppose not," I said. "Someone does have to collect the garbage."

"Sometimes I don't know how to take your words, Mr. Navarro."

"Lightly salted is the best way," I said.

"Oh, I see, but take my husband for instance, he works for the State Department too, and he has five chapters of a novel tucked away in a desk drawer. He's an artist at heart. He'd never make a good businessman."

"In that case, it's a good thing he's not in business."

"Yes, precisely, he ought to write more, but he just doesn't have the time. His job is so exacting."

"It's not easy," I said, and I extricated myself by pointing to my empty glass and heading back to the bar. I was halfway there when Mrs. Thompson intercepted me.

Chapter 3

M ARCO, WE MUST have our tête-à-tête. I'm so distraught. You're the only one who listens to me. Both my children treat me as if I were ready to be put out to pasture. Well, I'm not. For their sake I have to hang on. They haven't grown up. I have to be constantly after them to keep them out of trouble. I don't know why they've turned out this way. I did everything I could for them. You're like a son to me, Marco; you know that. I always hoped that you and Frannie... after your divorce, I mean... well, no sense talking about that now. I suppose Frannie is going to marry Larry Copland. Maybe it's all for the best. He'll be able to take care of her. She always wanted the kind of life he can provide. She craves it. I don't know how she got that way. We Thompsons have always been simple people. But Frannie, she's different. Maybe it was her father; he spoiled her you know. Of course you do. You know him well. I would have never guessed that you two would hit it off the way you did. The world is full of surprises."

Mrs. Thompson maneuvered me to a secluded alcove, and we sat down on the velvet cushions on a window seat. The park below was a mass of dark clumps. The river made an emphatic swath across the landscape, and on the far side, New Jersey lights, like the campfires of a besieging army, shone as constant reminders that indeed there was life beyond.

"It's Paul I want to talk to you about. There's nothing I can do about Frannie, not now at any rate. She's so obstinate.

But Paul is another story. All he needs is a little guidance, don't you think?"

"He's grown up, Bella. You have to let him go."

"It's not like that, Marco. It's not like that at all. He's really in trouble this time. He could get hurt."

Looking at Bella Thompson, I saw where Frannie got her looks. When young, Bella must have been a stunning woman. I liked Bella although sometimes taking her seriously was difficult. Still, there was something about her that impressed me—perhaps that she had survived a great deal, that she was spunky and always ready to fight back. She often surprised me with her ability to buck convention, though to look at her you would think she was the last person on earth who would march to a different drummer. Sometimes I didn't know whether I liked Bella because she was Frannie's mother or the other way around. Or maybe I just liked Bella because she liked me. I'm funny that way; I succumb to my admirers, especially when they are women.

We were both silent for a moment, and I could see her face soften. She was taking her mask off to take a minute respite. She turned her profile away from me. Her wisps of gray hair caught the light from the nearby lamp. When she turned back, she was again ready to take on the world—nose up and chin forward.

"He's involved with a horrible woman. Much older than he," she said.

"Oh, Bella!"

"It's not her age that I mind. I've been attracted to younger men myself." She knew that I knew that. "After all, men do it all the time. Get involved with younger women, I mean. Why shouldn't women do it too?"

"But not with your son."

"I didn't say that. But this woman is no good. For one thing, she's married, and her husband is violent."

21

"How do you mean, violent?"

"Well, he threatened to kill Paul."

"Irate husbands don't kill their wives' lovers anymore, Bella. Nowadays they're more likely to take the lover out for a drink, or better yet, they become tennis chums and meet at the club at six o'clock every morning. That's how they punish each other."

"You're not taking this seriously, Marco. Those things happen to men like you. People like Paul are likely to meet with terrible accidents."

She did have point. Paul was not the dashing type, though he did have some charm. Sometimes he tried my patience, something not easily done, I being akin to a saint in that respect. Still, they had taken me into their family, and I felt a certain responsibility towards them. I didn't have any siblings, and perhaps I hankered for that sort of relationship. The Thompsons offered me the opportunity to get as close as possible to fulfilling that. Of course, my feelings toward Frannie were definitely not brotherly.

"Everything you say may be true, Bella, but what can I do about it? I can't meddle in his private life."

"Just talk to him. He looks up to you. He'll listen to you. Please, Marco, do me this little favor. I may be in a position to put in a word for you in some other quarter."

Bella knew the chink in my armor, and she didn't hesitate to pry it with an empty promise. She was doing it for her offspring. The two of them were all she had—all that really meant anything to her. In this struggle, I was expendable, though I hardly thought that she realized how much I might be hurt. Perhaps I had played macho a little too convincingly, and now I had to pay the price. Or perhaps she really believed, or sincerely hoped, that what she was promising was a genuine possibility. That would certainly have put her mind at ease about Frannie.

"Well, who's this *femme fatale*, who's robbing your cradle? What's the secret of her fascination? And by the way, where is Paul? I haven't seen him tonight."

"Luckily, he's away this weekend. He had a concert in Boston. It came up after the party was all planned, and he's not one to miss a gig just to attend one of his sister's festivities. But that horrible woman is here. It's almost too much for me to bear."

"I don't understand."

"No, how could you? You never gave your mother such things to worry about. My children have made me prematurely gray. See if you can believe this: not only is he thrown together with this woman who's an actress, but it turns out that she's an old friend of Frannie's, who of course, refuses to cooperate with me. She insisted on inviting this friend tonight, and the brazen hussy shamelessly showed up. Can you top that? You just can't imagine the gall of some people, and she certainly knows how I feel about her. Her name is Sharon Hobart. She's somewhere around here. You can't miss her. She's wearing a slinky black dress."

"I think I already met her. Bella, you have nothing to worry about. Take my word for it."

"What makes you so sure?"

"What would a woman like that want with Paul? Haven't you blown whatever is between them out of all proportion?"

"I don't think so, Marco. You don't know her. She's like a snake. She'll strike where you least expect."

"I didn't know that was a characteristic of snakes."

"Well, whatever, you know what I mean."

"You say she's an actress, any good?"

"Some people think so."

"Stop worrying. Everything is going to be all right. I'll do what I can," I said, though the situation she had described seemed beyond my reach. I was certain that whatever, if

23

anything, was going on between Paul and Sharon would run its course and fizzle out harmlessly if it hadn't done so already.

Bella left me to fend for myself again, and I set out in search of Sharon. She was beginning to seem interesting. I spied her on the far side of the parlor. I made my way towards her through the throng of revelers. The number of bodies in the place had greatly increased since my arrival.

"Oh, there you are," she said linking her arm to mine. "I see you got rid of your guardian angel."

"Is that a way to speak about our hostess?"

"I only said she's an angel, isn't she?"

"She is."

"Oh, you have it bad. You need fresh air," she said pulling me towards the front door.

"Where are we going?"

"We're only one short flight from the roof garden. You're not afraid of heights, are you?"

"Not so you'd notice."

We climbed up the stairs. The door to the roof garden was open. A sign read: "Please remove high heels before stepping out." Sharon complied. "You see? I'm not as mean as I've been described."

"I didn't think so."

"Didn't you?"

"Would I lie to you?"

"Wouldn't you lie to anybody?"

"Of course not," I lied.

A few other people were hanging out on the terrace. Instinctively, we moved towards the shadows, as if we needed to be inconspicuous. Clouds drifted across the moon.

"Did you get the full story of my iniquities?"

"I heard about you and Paul."

"From the old lady, no doubt."

"What about it?"

"There's nothing to it. We're just friends. The kid needs friends. You must know that."

"What's in it for you?"

"I'm human too. I need people. We're both performers."

"You mean you make beautiful music together."

"Yes, we do."

I had never been particularly attracted to blonds, but I was beginning to feel that Sharon could be an exception. Everything seemed wrong about her, but in her presence I ceased to care about the facts. She wasn't at all like Frannie. This was a different kind of attraction. Sharon exuded earthiness. She reminded me of a pumpkin field at harvest time. I could smell her ripeness. There was nothing ephemeral about her. She radiated the reality of flesh and sweat. I couldn't touch her without retaining traces of it in my hands. She was the farmer's daughter, and to get to her one had to wade through the mud. I had an irresistible urge to get dirty.

The sounds of an altercation in the stairwell roused me from an ecstatic lull. I couldn't believe that anyone at that gathering was capable of creating a public disturbance. They were mostly from a class characterized by emotional constipation. But the sounds were unmistakable, someone loudly cursing.

"Oh, my God, that sounds like Joseph," Sharon exclaimed breaking away from me and heading for the stairs.

I followed her, vaguely suspecting who Joseph must be. At the bottom of the landing, by the Thompson's door, several corporate types were attempting to restrain a bearded young man who looked like he had just arrived, via time machine, from a 1960's coffeehouse.

He froze for a moment when he saw Sharon, but seeing me rekindled his anger. Breaking lose from his captors, he bounded up the stairs. Sharon threw herself in his path. He brushed her aside with enough force to bang her against the wall. She nearly toppled down the stairs but managed to keep her balance.

I had instantly surmised that Joseph wasn't coming up to shake my hand. I thought I could evade him until the two characters who had been holding him arrived to help me subdue him, but they seemed rather relieved to have him out of their hands and took their time to reengage.

Through the beard, Joseph's yellowing teeth presented a clenched determination. His eyes told me that reasoning with him would be useless. He swung with his right. I ducked. There wasn't much room to maneuver on the landing. He swung again. His fist met the wall directly behind me. His knuckles bled.

"Joseph, don't be crazy," Sharon threw her arms around his neck.

"Get away from me, bitch," he shoved her away. This time she tumbled. Luckily, the two clowns had gotten their act together. They managed to catch her before she hit the steps.

I was losing my patience with Joseph. He threw a headlock on me. I had no choice but to punch him in the ribs. I knocked the wind out of him with the first blow, but my blood was aroused. The palm of my hand shot out forcefully striking him between the eyes. He collapsed by the railing.

"Stop!" Sharon screamed. "Please, stop!"

I regained my senses. If only for a split second, I had been submerged in a primordial twilight where the instinct to kill is an automatic reflex.

"Oh, Joseph, Joseph, what am I going to do with you?" She was down by his side wiping the perspiration from his brow. She might have been lying at the bottom of the steps with a broken neck because of him. This is the essence of Christian charity, I thought.

"You know this guy?" one of the clowns asked. He wasn't directing the question at anyone in particular. I shrugged my shoulder.

"He's my husband," Sharon said unashamedly.

So this was the husband. I didn't know which of the two was more to be pitied.

"Joseph, Joseph, are you all right?" she tapped his face gently as he was coming to.

The commotion had enticed some of the guests out into the hall, Larry among them. He tried to usher everyone back into the apartment. The two corporate clowns had descended and tried to help Larry ride herd on the inquisitive crowd.

When Joseph regained consciousness, he burst into tears. He held on to Sharon like a penitent child. I didn't know what to make of it.

"Let's go home," she said to him. She helped him to his feet.

"I'll go down with you," I offered.

"No, it's all right, we'll manage," she said.

"I'll call a cab for you."

"No, really, we'll be all right."

I rang for the elevator and waited for it to come up. As she guided Joseph in, she surreptitiously squeezed my hand.

"Good night," I said.

She smiled weakly. Joseph nodded at me. I didn't think he remembered my face as the one he had just tried to bash. I stood there a few seconds after the elevator door closed, and I tried to pull myself together before going back to look for Frannie. I wanted to say good night to her also.

Chapter 4

A COUPLE OF DAYS after Frannie's shindig, I got an urgent call from Bella. Would I come up to see her as soon as possible? I agreed to be there that very afternoon. She would fix me a nice lunch, she said. Hamburger with cucumber wasn't exactly the greatest lunch, but Bella wasn't exactly a cook. I was grateful that she didn't overdo the burger.

Bella was her usual charming self. "You know Marc, you have to take care of yourself," she said as we munched on our lunch. "You don't look well at all." That was her way of preparing me for another assignment. This time it was Frannie I had to save. "You know," she continued, "marriage is not a step to be taken lightly. Nowadays people think it's such an easy thing to get a divorce that getting married hastily has become the norm. It's done or undone so easily, but it shouldn't be like that. If one could only pass one's experience on to one's children."

"That would be a feat," I said.

Bella sipped her cup of coffee, as she prepared for her attempt to get me involved.

"I was married to Henry for thirty-five years, before I decided I had enough," she said deciding against caution.

"Thirty-five years is a good chunk of time," I said matter-of-factly.

"What could I have done differently?" Bella asked rhetorically as if the fact were an indictment of her life.

Indeed, there was nothing that Bella could have done differently, or so it seemed to her at the time. She would have had to be a different person back then, at the very least the person whom she now was, or very nearly so in spirit. Hindsight has an essential hitch, a pitfall; looking back you mistakenly believe you see yourself, when in fact what you see is some distant predecessor.

So now Bella looked back to a time when she had been but a girl under the influence of a smothering family. She saw herself one spring evening walking hand in hand with a boy down the park path through the cherry blossoms. She remembered the curly black hair and intense eyes that begged her to seriously consider his love for her.

"I doubted myself," Bella said, "and so I made a mistake. I took my parent's advice and went with Henry, thirty-five years of a miserable marriage."

"Was it bad from the beginning?"

"It was bad from day one. It was bad even before that."

"There was no love, then?"

It was not an easy question for Bella to answer, though the answer was apparent. It was difficult to accept the facts, to own up to them so unequivocally. The question, like a spotlight aimed at dark corners, suddenly in full detail revealed objects that previously had been vague enough to allow interpretation. Memory sometimes seemed to be made up exclusively of dark corners that enable us to mitigate, by selective illumination, the discomfort of unpleasant recollections.

"I was in love once," she said, "but not with Henry."

She told me more about the boy with intense eyes and curly black hair under the cherry blossoms in the park. She remembered his face next to hers, and how she closed her eyes when their lips met. She no longer remembered the smell of him after so many years, but she remembered remembering that it had an extraordinary effect on her, and for a long time after, the memory of the texture of his lips and the smell of him so intoxicated her that she was afraid that she would unintentionally betray herself. She was never again able to achieve that feeling—with Henry or with anybody else. She could not even remember the feeling now, but only that she had cherished it. It was but a memory of a memory, the shadow of a shadow.

"It might have been different had I married Charles," she said.

"Why didn't you?"

Bella drew a deep breath, as if the answer to that question laid at the bottom of a deep lagoon, and she had to dive to retrieve it. "To put it simply," she said, "he was my cousin." She was up too soon to have plunged to the depth of the problem.

"I see," I said almost carelessly.

"It was my mother," Bella said, "who opposed it most vehemently." She paused for a moment, then added, "I suppose she meant well."

"And so you married Henry instead."

"That's the long and short of it," she said. "He was the darling of everyone. How could I resist?"

"Your life might have been different with your cousin," I said, "but not necessarily better."

"I'll never know, will I?"

"I suppose not," I said.

"The quandary is," Bella continued, "that I can't imagine a bad life with Charles, only the opposite."

"Well, what became of your cousin?"

"He married eventually, I heard. He's a veterinarian in Montana, or he was. Perhaps he's retired by now."

"Is that a life you would have wanted?"

"He loved horses."

"What about you."

"I loved him," she simply said as if that encompassed all possibilities. "Yes, and now there's Frannie. What do I do about Frannie?"

What to do about Frannie was always the question that hung over Bella, the parent, the overwhelming role in her life. The birth of her daughter had been a blessed event indeed, letting her slip out of the increasingly odious role of wife into the more acceptable one of mother. Acceptable, of course, didn't mean comfortable, for it was something she had to constantly reinvent. The constant wrestling with the question of what to do, in a sense having continually to adjust to the role, kept Bella jittery. It did, however, allow her, if not to escape completely, to keep at a greater distance from whatever was left of her matrimonial feelings.

Consciously or not she had raised Frannie to be her own person, and Frannie would do what she would do, as Bella well knew, regardless of what anyone else advised.

"I certainly see your problem," I said.

"Do you really?" Bella perked up, anticipation suddenly suffusing her face. The "seeing" of a problem was, after all, the beginning of arriving at a solution.

"Well," I continued, "must you do anything?"

"I can let her do whatever she wants, which is what I always do. But then, what becomes of my obligation as a mother?"

"What indeed?"

"I know she's making a mistake."

"Is she?"

"I can feel it in my bones."

"It's her mistake to make."

"Yes, but it's my duty to warn her. It's the most difficult thing to do, although it seems simple. You see, she will ignore the simple. She will have anticipated it and already discarded it. I have to warn her in a way she is not expecting, creative and subtle. Oh, how I hate that word, 'creative.' It's not simple at all. I have no idea, you know, where to go from here," Bella said, an indirect appeal for help that moved me.

"You just have to let her come to you," I said and wondered whether I was talking to Bella or to myself.

"Yes, but how on earth am I to manage that?"

"It will manage itself. All you have to do is wait."

"I suppose I have no choice," Bella said.

And neither had I.

"Marc, you're my last hope. Mr. T just refuses to help me with this." When she was disgruntled, she often referred to Henry as Mr. T. "The marriage isn't right. Frannie is not in love with that man. I can tell. I don't know why she's doing this."

"For money, for power, what's the difference? She's a grown-up. She has the right to do with her life whatever she wants."

"You're angry at her."

"I'm not angry. I'm just telling you what I see."

"You won't be much help if you're angry. I know she's not doing this to hurt you."

"There isn't much I can do."

"Yes, there is. She trusts you. You have to get it out of her—what the problem is. You have to find out."

"Bella, you don't know what you're asking."

"I thought you'd want to."

"I want to but I don't see how I can."

We heard the front door open then slam shut.

"Is that you Paul?" Mrs. Thompson called out.

"Who else could it be?" he shouted back from the kitchen. I heard the refrigerator door open.

Bella gave me a look as to indicate that this was an example of the kind of retort she had to put up with. Wasn't it a shame? A while back, Bella had asked me to keep a filial eye on Paul, and I took on that chore intending to make the best of it. Along the way, I tried to learn to play the role of big brother. The title sounded grand, sure to have some coveted privileges that I had yet to discover. The headaches were all too obvious. I decided to get better acquainted with Paul's activities. Knowing young people, having been one myself in the not too distant past, I figured I couldn't come on as an emissary from the bureau of parental authority. My approach would have to be a semi-undercover mission. So I tried to ease my way in as a lover of the arts by attending a performance of his jazz group.

The event took place in a basement in the East Village. A young man with dark curly hair sat at a table by the entrance apparently keeping an eye on the contribution box with a notice appended to it informing passersby that a five dollars contribution would be appreciated. I left a donation gladly enough, youth and art not to be denied.

I was early, not many people there yet. Those musical events tended to start late and the audience arrived accordingly. There was a makeshift stage at one end of the room and an odd assortment of benches scattered throughout the rest of the space. None looked very comfortable, or very clean. I looked around at the few people there, and indeed they all seemed barely out of high school. I made eye contact with a young lady across the room. She had dark hair cropped close to her ears, puffy cheeks, as if she had not yet shed her baby fat. Brash eye make-up, intended to proclaim her adulthood, but it merely accentuated her youth. I recognized her as the sort I had longed for when I was an adolescent. Times had changed. The tables were turned. Now, she was flattered that I looked at her, wished that I would give her a sign to approach. I wasn't even tempted.

The group played three sets with short intermissions between them, during which I took the opportunity to get acquainted with some of Paul's friends. The girl who had given me the eye then took a different tack and acted aloof. On learning that I was Paul's friend, she transferred her attention to him. He ignored her, no doubt already acquainted with her game, though to some he might have seemed unnecessarily cruel. She took it with exemplary fortitude.

After the performance, the musicians and some of the audience, mostly friends, moved to an upstairs apartment in the same building. The smoke came out, and I took a few drags. More people arrived. I was getting to see what school of fish he swam with. I sat on the couch and looked around the room, trying to find excuses for him; after all, boys will be boys. Cheryl, the girl with the large dark eyes sat next to me. Jet-black hair, black eyeliner, the dark motif was overwhelming.

"These parties are so boring," she said. She dragged on a joint and passed it to me.

"I suppose they become predictable," I said.

"Yeah," she said, "same people, same lingo."

"You could be home watching TV."

"I could," she agreed.

"I was kidding," I said. "All these people can't be tedious."

"You wanna bet?"

"No skeletons in the closets?"

"Plenty of skeletons, but who cares?"

"You must've been interested in something when you came here."

"Yeah, I was, foolish little me."

"Nothing risked, nothing gained," I said, as if that would console her.

"Are you up to anything more than giving advice? If you are, I'm interested."

"Right now I'm just comfortable sitting here."

"I should've known," she said. "You're like your friend."

"Like my friend?"

"Yes, Paul."

I took that to mean he wasn't interested in her either.

"I'm not lucky with men," she said.

"Is it luck?"

"It's the lack of it," she answered.

"I would think an attractive girl like you would make her own luck."

"Maybe I do," she said, "but it's all bad."

"What are you after?"

"Love," she said.

"That's reasonable."

"Yes, it is."

"I wouldn't despair, if I were you."

"I like Paul an awful lot."

"I'll put in a good word for you."

"It won't help," she said.

"Did you ever hear of the power of positive thinking?"

"Would you like to take me home?"

"I really can't."

"I know," she said.

I wondered what she really knew. Whatever it was, it seemed to appease her. She took heart, and she looked less sad than she had minutes before. Shortly after that conversation, I said good night to Paul and headed for home. I didn't sleep well that night.

I told Bella that I would do what I could about Frannie, but I knew Frannie well enough to realize that once she made up her mind about anything, it was no use trying to dissuade her.

Shortly Paul came into the room sipping a glass of milk and munching on a banana. "If this is a high level conference, just tell me and I'll leave," he said plopping himself down on a chair directly across from us.

"Nothing so serious," Bella said, "nothing serious at all."

She got up and left the room without another word. I stifled the impulse to follow her. If she were truly upset, letting her calm down would be better, and if she wasn't, playing her game made no sense.

"Don't worry, she's play-acting," Paul said. "She'll be back in a few minutes."

"Perhaps," I said dubiously.

"I know her," he assured me. "Hey," he exclaimed, remembering something. "Want to see what dear old dad sent Frannie for her birthday?" Without waiting for me to reply, he led the way down the hallway to the recreation room, where he stood at the door beaming.

I didn't see anything unusual. "Well?" I inquired.

"That," he said, pointing at the pool table.

"He sent her a pool table?"

"Neat, the old man has a sense of humor."

"I don't see the joke."

"Well, don't worry about it. Let's have a game."

I decided to go along. After all, that seemed to be my role with the Thompsons. He racked up and shot first scattering the balls pretty well. He had a lot of luck on that one. He sank five balls in a row, but I wasn't intimidated. I was pretty sure that I could take him, if I wanted to, although, in some remote fold of my psyche lurked a smidgen of doubt, small but disproportionately annoying, like a speck of dust under an eyelid. I'll shake it, I said to myself; I'll feel better after I sink a few. But I scratched after the second. It wasn't my day.

"Don't take it so hard," Paul gleefully said. "It's only a game."

I tried to smile, but my face felt stiff. I told myself to be reasonable. He was right. It was only a game. Nevertheless, losing wasn't easy for me. I don't suppose it's easy for anybody, but I always thought I could handle it. What bothered me the most was his enjoying it so much. His swagger got to me. It's his youth, I reasoned, why not be tolerant?

He chalked the cue and lined up. The seven sank into the corner pocket. He sank three more balls.

"I guess it's your day," I said.

"I suppose it is," he retorted with a smirk on his face.

He kept shooting without missing a single shot. No doubt about it, at the pool table, it was his day.

Chapter 5

Mr. Thompson was a partner in the brokerage firm Frisbee, McIntosh and Hobbs. A tall man with large hands, he looked more like a plumber than a Wall Street broker. He had a very subtle sense of humor of which he pretended to be unaware. He would introduce the most outrageous anecdotes into his ordinary conversation without the slightest cue that he was joking, and very often, his audience would continue on its merry way without an inkling that anything had been put over on them. I greatly admired that quality in Mr. Thompson, and I loved to watch him perform. But I only knew the surface manifestations of his character. It took me a while to notice the dark side of Henry Thompson.

His family wasn't as charmed by him as I was, though they rarely let on to that in those days. He took a liking to me beyond what I reasonably expected. Perhaps he wished that his firstborn had been a son. He didn't quite know how to relate to his offspring, as if for some reason he was afraid of them. Perhaps he feared their seeing through his façade of charm and proceed to expose him. Frannie and he weren't close, at least not then.

Mr. Thompson was a collector of rare books. One evening after dinner, he took me into his library under the pretense of showing me a leather bound first edition of *Wild Shrubs and Flowers of the Northern Islands*.

"I want to know, sir," he said to me as he turned the key in the bookcase lock, "what are your intentions toward my daughter?"

"I have no intentions," I hastily said.

His eyebrows jumped to his hairline.

"What I mean is that we're just friends. Frannie won't have it any other way."

"And you're going to put up with that?"

"I don't have a choice."

"Nonsense, Frannie is in love with you."

"Well, I don't quite see that."

He paused to consider for a moment. He had taken the book off the shelf and placed it on the reading table. Apparently, he had lost interest in showing it to me. "It's just as well," he said. "I don't really want you to get involved with Frannie. I like you too much. Frannie would try to turn you against me."

"She wouldn't," I protested. "Why would she? She's never shown the slightest inclination to disparage you."

"No, not yet," he said. "She's too smart. That's my Frannie, smart, but at her center she's cold and hard. I was cursed to have such a child. Beware of her."

I didn't know what to make of this outburst of hostility. I couldn't believe that a father would so vilify his own daughter. He read the disbelief in my face.

"Well, I speak in vain," he said. "Love is forever blind. You're a fine lad Marco, and I'm willing to help you with Frannie, even though it's against my better judgment. You have to look to your future, to your finances, because Frannie, as Romantic as she may sometimes seem, will never do without money. You may not be in a position right now take my advice, but when you're ready don't hesitate to ask, whether you're with Frannie or not."

"Thank you," I said having but a slight notion of what he was talking about.

"I don't suppose you're really interested in rare books and much less in rare flowers, are you?"

"No sir, not much," I said.

"Well then, let's have a drink and talk about politics."

We went back to the living room, and we didn't again allude to that conversation until my Aunt Petrina died leaving me a nest egg. At which time, Henry Thompson made good on his promise to help me.

Regularly, I got together with Henry on the golf course, even though I was piqued by the game's essential fault of requiring a great deal of artificially maintained ground. The ample allocation of resources to an activity engaged in by the few made the extravagance embarrassing to anyone with unimpaired sensibility. But seeing Henry Thompson amble down the fairway made the golf course seem a natural enough environment.

Henry didn't have a philosophical bent, so he seldom ruminated about his surrounding or his place in it. His presence continually transformed his surroundings. If he was comfortable in a place, he enjoyed it; if not, he changed it. Like a river, he wore down what didn't move. He couldn't be denied, and either he flowed around obstacles, or he overwhelmed them when he had to.

"It's not as if I have much leeway," I said trying to feel my way towards a proper attitude, though proper for what escaped me.

"It's not as if you need much," Henry responded.

"Is that the issue, then, what I need?"

"Isn't that always the issue? What everyone needs?"

"Well, then what does Frannie need?"

"That, you'll have to ask her."

"Isn't she telling us loud and clear? She's made her choice."

"You don't have to worry about Frannie's choices. She'll do that for herself. The question is, what's your choice?"

I had convinced myself, and I wanted to continue believing, that I had no choice about Frannie. Henry Thompson thought otherwise. He believed in grabbing the bull by the horns, assuming that one wanted to wrestle the bull. But what then, after the bull was down in the dust? Cowboys just stood up and walked away. For them, it was only a brief contest, but I saw no walking away. For me, the problem became holding the beast down forever. Only the mythical proportions of such a prolonged struggle was noteworthy; as arduous as the twelve labors of Hercules with one difference, the task had yet to elevate anyone to the pantheon of the demigods. The complexity of the question prevented an immediate answer. It seemed to me that the world no longer recognized domestic heroism, that stealing fire from heaven would no longer be an affront to whatever gods where left. So who would notice the struggle of a man holding a bull by its horns down to the ground, even for a lifetime? Only the man would be aware of the lonely act. The value of his life would depend on his own will to believe in himself.

I slowly approached the ball already on the green. The putt wouldn't be as easy as Henry suggested but still possible. I crouched to get a better sense of how the grass napped between the ball and the hole. Even the best shot in golf doesn't always make it, but you always take the shot, the difference, I supposed, between a game and real life.

Chapter 6

SEVERAL WEEKS AFTER Frannie Thompson's party, I received a card in the mail announcing the opening of a play at the Lower East Side Playhouse. I immediately wrote it down in my calendar, although these neighborhood theater productions are often hard to take. The acting has to be really terrific to overcome the general shabbiness of the sets and the rest of the would-be-theater surroundings. Occasionally, the opposite happens, and by some fluke the production manages to get a talented person to put a terrific set together, and the actors under the influence of a dreadful director prance about the stage without the slightest notion of what the author had in mind. I remember just such an event at the Village Repertory Theater, with a production of *Ana Kleiber*. The set got rave reviews, and everything else was panned. Well, I was ready to deal with that, because this time Sharon Hobart had the leading role, and just to see her, I was willing to put up with a great deal.

I found my way to the theater easily enough. The architect had made an attempt to keep it from having that institutional look of public schools and housing projects, but he had failed. Cinder blocks were not immediately visible, but I had the overwhelming feeling that a wall of massive concrete blocks would greet me around the next corner.

Posters all over the place advertised the production. I paid the admission charge at the door, and I shuffled into the auditorium along with a group of elderly ladies who had suddenly appeared. Early yet and the house not full, there were still a few empty seats in the front row. I headed for one of them to sit where nothing would obstruct my view of Sharon. The starting time passed, and twenty minutes later the audience was beginning to fidget, finally the lights dimmed and the curtain went up.

Sharon was playing the lead in Ibsen's *Hedda Gabler*, but I didn't really care what play was being performed. I came to the theater to see Sharon. She was impressive enough, and I got more than I expected. The minute she uttered her first line I knew I was in for something. Sharon knew that part. She knew it well enough to make me uncomfortable.

Hedda had created a predicament from which she couldn't extricate herself. I wondered whether in her own life Sharon had done the same. Did she really love her husband? I had to figure that out if I was to play my part as well as she played hers. But what was my part? Certainly I wasn't an Ejlert, the genius with a weakness for alcohol, and for women too, I suppose. Judge Brack was certainly a disgusting character, but his coming on to Hedda seemed uncomfortably familiar. Wasn't that where I was heading with Sharon?

Maybe she had thought this all out, and that's why she had invited me to see her perform. Or maybe, just like any typical person, I was ascribing more meaning to random happenings than they actually had, if they had any at all. I didn't know what I was getting myself into. My reason told me that I was headed in the wrong direction, but there wasn't much I could do about it. Whatever drives a man and a woman together is beyond reason. I wished that weren't the case, but there was nothing I could do about it. Or maybe I'm just making an excuse for myself.

If Sharon was trying to tell me what kind of trouble lay ahead, I wasn't about to heed the warning. Perhaps Sharon wasn't the one trying to look out for me. Maybe we all have a guardian angel to warn us of impending danger, and we have a choice of heeding the warning or ignoring it. Of course, that view sounds too optimistic, but maybe we need that belief to get through life's uncertainties. There are too many random probabilities to comfortably predict the consequences of every action. Sitting in the darkness of the theater, I watched that beautiful if enigmatic woman deliver a performance that made her all the more irresistible. She was interesting, but even more so, she was desirable, one quality inseparable from the other.

After the lights came on again and Sharon got up from the sofa on which Hedda had shot herself, the applause increased. I considered standing up and shouting "bravo," but I restrained myself. The applause died down and people began to exit. I stayed in my seat, as did some others who I presumed were friends of members of the cast and like me waited to personally deliver accolades. In about fifteen minutes, Sharon emerged from backstage in her street clothes. Yellow sweater, tight jeans, she was ready to play another part.

I was about to wave to her to assure my presence was noted, but several other people surrounded her before I had a chance. As I waited my turn in the background, the guy who played Ejlert came out. He seemed less interested in the compliments thrown his way than in conveying some message to Sharon. She shook her head and made a slight sign toward me. Chagrin suffused his face as he looked my way. It's always a pleasure to elicit that kind of reaction from a competitor, and I'm as competitive as the next guy. She stepped up to me and whispered in my ear, "Want to leave?" I was ready. She said good night to those around her, and we were off. Ejlert stared after us quite crest fallen.

"I feel like dancing," she said. "Let's go to an unpretentious place."

"I know just the spot."

It took us no time to drive uptown.

She was a little taken aback when we entered the place. The bar area was completely done in art deco—the high ceiling and the walls covered from top to bottom with glass, etched with tall delicate floral designs on the edges; the bar top and tables, black marble; and all the wood, polished mahogany accented with chrome. The place was hopping.

"I thought we were going to a simple place," she said mockingly.

"These places don't come in the simple variety," I explained. "There are grungy ones, though. What will you drink?" I asked.

"Gin and tonic."

I ordered a gin and tonic and bourbon straight up. The luminescent dance floor beckoned. We sipped our drinks for a minute, and we were ready to go. Sharon was a dream dance partner. She responded to every move effortlessly. We danced like two bodies with one mind soaking up the music. It passed through us like electricity running through a cable, except that we gave it expression. We became the music, and we made it visible. I was so happy to move with her, to touch her, to hold her! I began to fear that something evil was about to happen. My high was too high. A crash would be stupendous. I caught myself sounding like an old man. I admonished myself and repressed my apprehensions.

On our way back to the table we ran into a couple of Sharon's friends. A wave of annoyance rippled over her face, but it quickly dispelled. She introduced me. The two strangers, a man and a woman, professed to be charmed to make my acquaintance. They looked familiar, but I was sure I had never met either one of them before, not formally anyway. The man said something about "Charles" being there also.

"How nice," Sharon replied, "I'm always glad to see dear old Charles." She dragged me to our table. "The trouble with places like this," she said, "is that one is bound to run into people like that."

"They look familiar, but I can't place them."

"They both work for Allied Chemicals. You must have seen them at Frannie's party."

"Ah, yes but they weren't there together, were they?"

"He was there with his wife. This one is his girl Friday, but she works a seven day week, if you know what I mean."

"You disapprove?"

"Heaven forbid. I can't afford to disapprove."

"People have been known to live beyond their means."

"Let's go somewhere else," she said, "right now."

That was all right with me. We were getting up to go when a man approached us and asked Sharon to dance.

"I'm afraid we don't have time," I said to him in my most elegantly hostile manner.

"It's all right," Sharon said, "Marco, this is Charles."

He shook my hand without smiling. His eyes seemed focused on an unspecified point over my right shoulder. He led Sharon to the dance floor. I sat down to wait and finish my drink. A couple of uninvited birds sat at my table. I ignored them and they left. It dawned on me that I was pissed at Sharon for having gone off with Charles. Who was this Charles anyway? I got up to go look for them. They didn't seem to be on the dance floor.

Finally, I saw them on the other side. They seem to be arguing. Sharon turned to walk away, but he grabbed her arm. Through the crowd, I started making my way towards them. By the time I got across, Charles had disappeared, lucky for him. I would have killed him. Visibly shaken, Sharon was leaning up against a pillar. She recoiled as I approached her.

"I'll be in the ladies room," she said, walking away.

I followed her and waited near the door. I kept my eyes

peeled for Charles, but he didn't show. Sharon came out looking more composed. "Are you all right?" I asked.

"Yea, I'm all right," she said.

I looked at her questioningly. She couldn't take it. Her defenses crumbled. She threw her arms around me.

"Hold me," she said.

The lights had dimmed. A slow number was on. She had me on the dance floor. I had no will.

"Take me somewhere," she whispered.

This time I wasn't going to let anybody interfere. I had parked the car at a garage around the corner from the club. As we walked in that direction, we heard a shout from the other side of the street. We turned to see a figure dashing across toward us. A couple of fellows were apparently chasing him, but they retreated into the shadows when they saw Sharon and me.

The running figure didn't make it across the street. A speeding car suddenly appeared. The sound of flesh on metal was louder and more horrifying than I would have predicted. The body slid about forty feet. The vehicle had made no discernible attempt to stop before impact and certainly made none afterward. We ran toward the victim as a crowd gathered, humans, like sharks, attracted by blood. From the periphery of the crowd, we saw the victim's face. It was Charles. I heard the sirens approaching. Someone must have dialed 911.

"Let's get out of here," Sharon said tugging my sleeve.

"We ought to wait for the police," I said.

"Let's not get involved," she said. "There's nothing we can do anyway."

I saw that she meant it—that she had a reason for wanting to leave in a hurry. That was just as well. There wasn't much information I could give the police. I didn't get the license number or the make of the car. All I knew was that it was a dark sedan.

We walked away. "I'll take you home now," I said.

"I don't want to go home," she said.

"My place," I suggested.

"Fine," she said.

On the way down, I restrained myself from asking any questions about Charles. I had a feeling that before long she would tell me more than I wanted to know. We dropped the car off at the garage, and then walked across the street and down the block to Fifth Avenue. Molloy, the night doorman, was on. I was glad. He wasn't as talkative as Max. Molloy restricted his conversation to, "Good evening," or "Good morning," or to some innocuous remark about the weather.

The accident having put a damper on things, the evening wasn't turning out quite the way I hoped.

"You want a drink?"

"Sure," she said. She looked around the place.

I fixed her a gin and tonic.

"If you're not a bestselling author, how do you manage all this—the Mercedes, the address, the art work?"

"Let's not get into that now," I said.

"What do you want talk about? You want to talk about Charles?"

"Only if you do," I said.

"I don't."

"All right."

"I suppose you want to get right down to sex."

"Only if you do."

"Don't you have any wishes of your own?"

"I'm saving those," I said.

"You're a prick, you know that. You think a clever remark will save you from everything."

"I'll take you home," I said.

"I don't want to go home," she screamed. Tears burst from her eyes. She sobbed uncontrollably. I stifled my impulse to hold her. I watched her cry for a few minutes.

"I'm sorry," she said wiping the tears and smudging her makeup. "I must look awful."

"You look fine," I said.

"Let me stay here tonight," she said. "I don't want to be alone."

"Sure," I said. I wondered about Joseph's whereabouts, but I didn't ask. "You can have my bedroom. I'll sleep here."

"I don't want to throw you out of your own bed." She seemed genuinely concerned.

"It's very comfortable here," I assured her. I showed her where everything was. The master bedroom had a bathroom of its own.

I came back to the living room with bedding for myself. I pushed several of the modular pieces together to make a bed. I undressed down to my birthday suit, pulled down a copy of Plato's Republic, and crawled into bed. I read a couple of chapters, but I really had a hard time keeping my mind on what I was reading. After all, the description of the physical world as merely a shadow of reality is hard to swallow. I had yet to become enlightened. My mind kept wandering into the other room. I put out the light and tried to sleep. It was no use. I was too worked-up. My eyelids were heavy but the rest of me refused to let them shut. I was finally about to doze off when I felt the covers being lifted. She slid in next to me.

"I heard you thrashing about," she said.

"I couldn't sleep."

"Neither could I," she confessed.

I was glad. Her body was firm and warm next to mine. She made love even better than she danced.

We slept very late the next morning. When I first opened my eyes, I was startled to find myself in the living room. Then I remembered the events of the previous night. I looked at the mass of blond hair on the pillow beside me. It was Sharon's all right. I got up, went to the bathroom, shaved and washed up. I peered into the living room on my way to the kitchen. She was still there, still sleeping. In the kitchen I made a pot of coffee, but that's all the breakfast I could come up with. There were no eggs in the refrigerator and only two slices of stale whole wheat bread. I wondered why the housekeeper hadn't done the shopping. She was a wonderful woman, kept the place spotless, but sometimes she forgot things. I had to talk to her about that. Or maybe I was the absent minded one and had forgotten to leave money for the groceries.

I poured two cups of coffee put them on a tray along with a creamer and a sugar bowl and brought everything out to the living room. I watched Sharon sleep while I sipped my coffee. She began to rouse. Suddenly she was brilliantly awake. She smiled, stretched and sat up in bed.

"Coffee?" I offered.

"Breakfast in bed! What service!"

"It's not quite breakfast," I said. "It's only coffee. The cupboard is otherwise bare."

"I forgot my toothbrush."

"You can use one of mine."

"Okay, I'll be right back."

She leapt out of bed. The cupboard wasn't the only thing bare in my apartment. But where one was a lack, the other revealed overwhelming bounty. I heard the water running in the shower and then stop.

"I need a bathrobe."

"There are plenty in the closet," I shouted.

I heard the closet door slide open and shut. She came

back into the room wearing one of my bathrobes. It was a little large on her, but she wore it with élan. The bathrobe would never want to be on me again.

"This coffee is not as warm as it used to be," I said. "I'll get you a fresh cup."

"Nah, I like it tepid," she said. She took the cup and sipped. "It's plenty hot," she said. "You've been up for a while. You shaved and washed already and made the coffee."

"All that didn't take very long," I said. "I wanted to sit here and watch you sleep for a long while, but you got up too soon."

"Oh, so you like to spy on ladies while they sleep," she said gleefully.

"Some ladies," I explained. "Some ladies do everything exquisitely."

"Yes, some do," she said losing her smile. "Do you think I'm a terrible woman?" she asked, as if suddenly reminded of a childhood memory.

I lost my equanimity for a moment. I didn't know whether she was joking. "I think you're wonderful," I said, but that wasn't what she wanted to hear.

"I'm serious," she said. "You think I'm terrible, don't you?"

"No," I said. I really meant it.

"I'll make it up to you. I'll make you like me."

"I like you already."

"You don't know me. The way I really am, I mean."

"Everything I know about you I like," I said.

"I'll be everything you want me to be. I promise."

"Be yourself, that's enough."

"Love me," she said, throwing her body against mine.

I had no choice. I didn't want any. Afterward, I felt drained. There is a calmness after making love that is always disappointing. Fulfillment in anything, I suppose, is always somewhat of a letdown—never compares favorably with the tension of expectation. I needed something to get me going again. I felt hungry.

"Let's go to Feathers," I said. "They have the greatest croissants."

"Okay," she said. Then she seemed to remember that she wasn't home. "All my clothes got sweaty at the dance last night. I wish I had something else."

"Maybe we can dig something up," I said. We went down the corridor to the back closet where I kept the Lost and Found.

"You're amazing!" she exclaimed. "You keep dresses around for moments like these! Do you have several different sizes or do all the women who stay here overnight look approximately the same?" Her shift into sarcasm was too smooth for comfort.

"Women don't seem to be able to help leaving articles of clothing behind. Even my wife left a few things."

"So you're married," she said. That seemed to amuse her a great deal.

"Divorced," I said.

"That's a mere technicality," she quipped.

"You must be a Catholic," I said.

She didn't respond to that. She looked through the four or five dresses.

"Why don't you have a stoop sale?" she said.

"Retail isn't my forte," I answered truthfully. "Besides, I don't think my neighbors would appreciate it."

She picked a dress, and retired into the bedroom where she had left the rest of her garments the night before. My blood began to pulse again as I followed her. I could describe her physical attributes, but that would not convey her beauty. It wasn't her flesh, or the color of her skin, unusually dark for a blond, or the way she moved, or the way she dressed or undressed, but all of that together and something more. The something more was the crucial factor. She seemed at her physical peak, and she would age well. The image of her walking down the gray blue corridor in her bare splendor would stay with me for a long time.

Chapter 7

THE DAY AFTER SHARON'S death was headline in the papers, I got a call from Lt. Romanelli. "We're investigating the death of Sharon Hobart," he said on the phone. "Do you mind if we come down and ask you a few questions?"

"How about if you ask me the questions now, save yourself a trip," I said.

"Nah, I want to see you in person," he said, "eyeball to eyeball, nose to nose."

"How about three o'clock," I suggested in my iciest tone.

"How about earlier," he said.

"I can't make it before three," I said.

I wanted to cooperate fully with the endeavor to apprehend Sharon's killer, but there was something about Romanelli's tone that triggered a defensive reaction. He sounded like the kind of guy who likes to steam-roll over people just for the hell of it. I imagined him chomping on a cigar.

In person though, he didn't look like that at all. For a cop, he was thin, his face almost pretty, head covered with a shock of curly black hair. He reminded me of Vinnie Caravaggio, the best looking boy in my junior high school. All the girls were gaga over Vinnie, and when two of his front teeth were knocked out in a baseball accident, you would have thought he was a tragic hero the way they carried on. I looked at Romanelli's mouth for signs of restoration of his front teeth. He must have had a good dentist; his teeth looked natural, and he had the swagger of someone who considered himself attractive to women. He also thought himself a smart guy.

His partner, Stephen Oblonsky, was a different type

altogether. Perhaps they had agreed that Oblonsky would play the tough guy and Romanelli the suave one. Anyway, Oblonsky had the look that went with unsophistication. Or maybe he wasn't acting at all. There are plenty of those guys out there for real and doubtlessly more than a few in the police force. Oblonsky was the taller of the two, and he had a military style haircut, no hair on the sides and extra short on top.

They both walked into my apartment seemingly cool. Oblonsky didn't see anything that wasn't directly in front of him, and what he saw he ignored. Romanelli had a hard time trying to hide the fact that he was impressed with the layout. The living room was designed for comfort, everything plush, the colors subdued. Several paintings betrayed my taste for the post-impressionists. Romanelli looked at them very carefully.

"You get a kick out of this?" he inquired.

"Art soothes me," I said.

"I'll bet it does."

"Can I offer you gentlemen something to drink, scotch, bourbon, Perrier?"

They both declined.

"Tell us about Sharon Hobart," Romanelli said.

We all sat down. Oblonsky sat at the edge of an armchair and stared at me. He didn't say a word.

"She was a friend of mine," I said, "a good person."

"I suppose you knew her well enough," Romanelli said.

"I suppose I did," I replied. I had to watch my step with him. He resented me already. He figured I never had to deal with the street. He figured I inherited everything I had. I might have felt the same way had I been in his place, but that didn't make his hostility less irritable.

"How long did you know her?" he asked.

"Not long," I said.

"What was the nature of your relationship?"

"Like I said, we were friends."

"That's all?"

"Isn't that enough?"

"What I mean is, how well did you know her?"

"Well enough," I said.

"We're not getting anywhere, are we?"

"Maybe we will, if you tell me what you're after."

"I'm after a suspect. I'm after someone with a motive to kill her."

"You mean, you don't think it was a random killing. You don't think it was just a psycho with a taste for theater."

"It probably was, but I want to check every angle."

"What about those 'significant clues' mentioned in the paper?"

"We're looking into those."

"But you're not at liberty to reveal them."

"That's right."

"But they do really exist."

"That's right too."

"Well then, what do you want from me?"

"How often did Sharon Hobart visit this apartment?"

"Now and then, the way friends do."

"Was she here the day she was killed?"

"No, as a matter of fact, we hadn't seen each other for several weeks."

"You had quarreled?"

"Not exactly. We had a philosophical disagreement."

"I suppose you can account for your whereabouts on the night of the murder."

"I certainly can. That's my poker night."

"Life would be a lot easier for all us if you cooperated with this investigation. When was the last time Mrs. Hobart came to these premises?"

That was a weak bluff, but I decided to go along. Why not? He wasn't as smart as I first thought. We both knew that I could make life tougher for him than he could for me.

"About three weeks ago," I said.

"Well, back then did she tell you anything that might have led you to believe she was in danger?"

"No, nothing at all," I said.

"And you're certain she wasn't here any time after that."

"I'm reasonably certain."

"To the best of your knowledge, was she involved in any criminal activities?"

"To the best of my knowledge, she certainly wasn't."

Oblonsky opened his mouth for the first time. "You're a wise guy, Navarro," he said in a monotone. He didn't elaborate.

The abruptness of the utterance startled me. I sensed that those words had exhausted his insight, if not his vocabulary. This pair disappointed me. They seemed to have stepped out of a television sitcom about two idiots who decide to impersonate detectives. I pretended that the remark had come from Romanelli. I glimpsed my reflection in his eyes. "I can afford to be one," I said. He knew what I meant.

"We're not trying to hassle you, Navarro, but we got a job to do, and we're going to do it. Regardless of how much pull you have downtown, it doesn't put you above the law."

He was getting nervous. When cops get nervous they get tough. I didn't want to push him over the edge. No sense in making unnecessary enemies. I tried to make a conciliatory statement. "You're right," I said. "I'm sorry. Is there anything else you want to know?"

"What about Joseph Hobart? What do you know about him?"

"Not much. He's a sculptor. Not bad at all."

"Does he make money at it?"

"Does anybody? He teaches classes now and then. What does his financial situation have to do with this?"

"Well, if he didn't make any money, then she must've been supporting him."

"Maybe, I wouldn't know. People in the theater don't make all that much money either, unless they make it big. Sharon hadn't reached that stage yet, pardon the pun."

"That's what I'm driving at. They must have had some other source of income, don't you think?"

"That sounds reasonable but not necessarily sinister. Her family has money."

"We already checked that. They had cut her off completely. They didn't even talk to her."

I was already aware of that, but I wasn't comfortable with the innuendoes. The bare facts didn't really provide a true picture of her. I'll be the first to admit that she was no angel, but down at the core, despite of everything, she was one hell of a good human being. That's the way I wanted to remember her, and I resented a stranger besmirching her memory. But she really didn't need my protection anymore. When she did need it, I wasn't able to provide it. That's a hard thing for a man to accept—failing to protect someone he loves.

"So what's your theory?" I asked.

"She's bringing in the dough, and he's taking it easy sculpting away. She gets tired of that, starts fooling around with you. He sees his meal ticket evaporating, gets nervous and kills her."

"That doesn't make sense, Romanelli, and you know it. If she was the meal ticket, why would he kill her?"

"I'm not saying he was rational. Maybe he didn't even mean to kill her. Maybe it was an accident. Maybe, he only wanted to scare her."

"If you think he's the killer, why aren't you down there questioning him?"

"We already questioned him. He acts guilty as hell."

"But you have no evidence…"

"He's got an alibi. It checks out."

"But you still think he's got a motive, and he acts guilty…"

"Maybe he didn't do it, but then again, maybe he did."

"And then again, maybe I did it," I said.

"Maybe you did. We're going to find out."

He was grinning now. I had an impulse to punch him in the face, but I decided to bide my time.

"We'll be seeing you," Romanelli said as they got up to go. Oblonsky barely nodded his head as he followed his partner out.

There was something screwy here. I didn't think Romanelli believed the cock-and-bull story about Joseph being the killer. Nobody could be that obtuse. On the other hand, maybe cops were especially dense. Sometimes it was hard to tell. I hadn't the faintest idea why he came down to see me, and that bothered me. He was up to something, but what? Maybe he was just fishing for clues. Maybe those significant clues mentioned in the papers were not that significant. But then again, he didn't ask me that many questions about Sharon, and the ones he asked were somewhat off-the-wall. There really wasn't much he wanted to know about Sharon. Not that there was much I could have told him that would have been helpful. Sharon liked to take chances, and that probably contributed to the tragedy. But that was also a quality that had made her exciting.

Chapter 8

AFTER ROMANELLI AND Oblonsky left, I sat at my desk and mulled over The Wall Street Journal—dry stuff. I could have left my money in the bank and lived comfortably on the interest for the rest of my life, but somehow that seemed decadent, not quite the manly thing to do. So, I kept stalking the deals, always looking for the big score, and once in a while, among all the little ones that were ultimately the mainstay, there was the big one that made me feel like a big game hunter, but that wasn't helping me at the moment.

I tried to do some work. I was concentrating on a series of stories about a gang of boys growing up in the Bronx. My ideas for stories were always great—the concept always exciting, the characters wonderful—they were always real characters, people I remembered from my youth. The problem was that when I got everything down on paper it all seemed flat. Typing had knocked the life out of it. But I didn't want to give up. I knew I had stories to tell. The setting was colorful, and as I said, the characters were real and vibrant in my imagination, but I couldn't make it all come alive on paper.

Of course, maybe I was too preoccupied with Sharon's death. In the back of my mind, the event lurked unceremoniously, an annoying buzz around my head, like a fly that wouldn't go away or a mosquito in the middle of the night. But somehow I didn't really believe that she was dead. I still expected to pick up the phone and hear her voice at the other end. I kept thinking of how much I had enjoyed taking her out to dinner. She liked small out-of-the-way places in

Little Italy. Several times she dragged me out to restaurants in Brooklyn. I would gladly walk barefoot to Sheepshead Bay right now if only she were there waiting for me.

"She's dead," I said to myself, "you have to face it." But I couldn't believe it. How could that be? This wasn't supposed to happen to me. I used to wonder, when I read stories of similar incidents in the paper, about the people close to the victim. What were they feeling? What were they doing? How were their lives changing? I never imagined that I would be one of those people and that someone else might think about me in curious anonymity.

My father had died, but that was a long time ago, when I was a child. I didn't remember him anymore. I saw pictures of him in his army uniform, and guided by the photographs, I manufactured memories of him, but when I tried to remember him in some other way, as a civilian, I drew a blank. That's how I knew that I didn't remember him really—that I made up the memory because I wanted to remember my father. His death was a vague event in my life, a long drawn out development. Growing up was the process of realizing that he would never return.

Sharon's death was something else, a definite event in the present, an event in the news. A death couldn't get more official. Yet, I tried to live my life the way I had always lived, and I was surprised that I was able to do so—surprised that the elevator stopped at the sixteenth floor when I pushed the appropriate button, surprised that the car started when I turned the ignition key. None of that was affected by Sharon's death. That was a mystery to me. As I sat pondering my morbid condition, the phone rang. It was Frannie Thompson at the other end.

"Hello, Marc, I'm sorry to disturb you. I know what you must be going through."

"I'm all right," I said, thinking that there was no way she could possibly know what I was feeling.

"I'm having a little bit of a problem down here."

"Down where?"

"At Joseph Hobart's loft," she said, as if I were supposed to understand what she was doing there. "He needs help, Marc. He's not well. Didn't Sharon tell you?"

"Tell me what?"

"Marc, really, I need you. Will you get here?"

That sounded like an order, and I didn't like it. But my curiosity prevailed. "I'll be down right away," I said. "What's the address?" I knew the address, but I didn't want Frannie Thompson to be sure of that. I wanted to keep her guessing—keep her off balance until I was sure of her. I caught myself in the middle of this thought. Of what did I want to be sure? Why did I distrust Frannie? Because I didn't know what she was doing with Joseph Hobart? That was a perfectly reasonable place for her to be after Sharon's death. They had been friends, after all, but something told me to stay on the alert. Perhaps Sharon was looking after me from the other world. I was losing my grip, succumbing to sentimentalism. I had to get a hold of myself and stay sane.

"One-o-seven Green," she said. "You'll have to walk up. The elevator is out of order."

I knew the exact location. I'd been there with Sharon, once when Joseph was away. He seemed to be away intermittently for weeks at a time. The place was a nice loft that Sharon had bought when she first came to New York and her parents were still supporting her.

When I got there, Frannie answered the door. Her face drawn, she looked somewhat disheveled—for Frannie that is—in a faded cotton suede shirt, that had been orange when new, and designer jeans that fit like a second skin. She always looked thinner than the image suggested by the number that came up when she stood on a scale. I never ceased to be surprised, when I put my arms around her, at how much of her there really was.

Her look clashed with the Hobart surroundings. The wall opposite the front entrance had been stripped of all plaster and the brick refinished to elicit a strong sense of bare reality. On it hung several antique pieces that had been thoughtfully acquired. An oak desk occupied the corner opposite the entrance. Over the desk hung an antique clock; its mechanism apparently no longer functioned, or someone had forgotten to rewind it. Turning to the right, the room receded with a large space, along the side some more antiques—a chest and a wicker baby carriage that made me wonder whether Sharon had been looking forward to someday putting it to practical use. That space ended with a shelving structure that held fancy pieces used only on special occasions and behind that the dining area followed by the kitchen. There was a sitting area to the right, and above it jutted the upper level that contained the bedrooms. Proceeding to the rear, a narrow hallway led to the bathroom on the left, and on the right, a door led to Joseph's studio.

"I'm so glad you're here," she said in her sincerest tone. She grabbed on to my arm. She knew that I loved to be needed.

Suddenly, there was a flurry of pounding on a nearby door. Joseph shouted to be let out—rather, he was threatening to kill Frannie if she didn't let him out.

"What's going on?"

"I managed to lock him in there," she said triumphantly.

"You locked him up?" I was flabbergasted.

"He didn't take his medication, and that makes him crazy."

Joseph kept making a god-awful racket to be let out, and Frannie wasn't making anything clearer.

"Frannie, what is going on here?" I had a sudden desire to bolt for the street.

"I can't believe Sharon never mentioned this to you," she lowered her voice as if she were going to tell me a secret. "Don't you know that Joseph is ill? Sometimes he gets crazy, violent even, and he has to take medication."

"What the-hell are you doing here, Frannie?"

"He called me. He said he needed somebody to be with him for a little while. He felt a bout of depression coming on. That's part of the symptoms too. With Sharon gone, I thought it was the least I could do. But when I got here, he started ranting and raving about how I know perfectly well why Sharon was killed, and that I know who killed her. First, I didn't know what to make of it, but then I remembered that he's supposed to be taking medication, and if he doesn't take it, he goes over the edge. I told him I don't know what he's talking about. I think I managed to convince him a little, but he's still distraught. He thinks Sharon's death is part of a conspiracy."

"Frannie, you're out of your mind. He's just going to be more upset to see me here."

"No, he won't. Not for the reason you think, anyway. He's not like that. And what difference does it make? Sharon's dead. You can both love her now without conflict."

Joseph banged on the door as if trying to break it down.

"Well, why did you lock him up if he was so calm?"

"He started again to talk about how I know who the killer is, and that I better tell him. I tricked him into going in there, and I locked the door. I figured that was the safest thing to do till you got here."

"He threatened you physically?"

"Well, I wasn't sure what he might do. He looked like he wasn't exactly in control."

I didn't have time to be angry with Frannie. Joseph had

descended into a different stage of hysteria. I heard his body slump to the floor as he cried hysterically.

"Oh God, I feel so awful," Frannie said.

I didn't quite believe her, though she had the sincerest expression on her face. "We better let him out," I said.

Frannie gave me the key. When I opened the door, Joseph didn't move. He lay in a heap, like a straw man whose support had snapped in several places. I lifted him up and dragged him to the couch. "Get some water," I said to Frannie. She fetched it from the kitchen. I got Joseph to drink some. Brandy would have been better, but I wasn't sure it would go with his medication, if it was true that he was taking any.

"Take it easy, Joseph. Everything is all right," I said. He seemed dazed. I wasn't sure he knew where he was or who was talking to him. "Everything is all right," I repeated.

He shook his head. "No," he said, without defiance or anger. He seemed sad and resigned.

"Listen, Joseph are you ill? Is there something we can do for you?"

He shook his head.

"Can we call your doctor?"

"No," he said.

"I have the number," Frannie said.

I wondered why she hadn't called the doctor in the first place.

"She's dead," he said.

"Who?"

"She knows who did it," he said pointing to Frannie.

She shrugged her shoulders in baffled denial.

"Nobody knows," I said. "The police don't know. We don't know."

He shook his head. "Coffee," he said. He was becoming alert. "I need some coffee to wake me up."

"I'll make it," Frannie said.

I would have guessed that she didn't know how, but I was wrong that time. She made a good pot of coffee. While Frannie was making the coffee, Joseph kept telling me that Sharon's death was part of a plot. He couldn't tell quite what the plot was, but Charles had been involved. He was dead too. That seemed to be his only proof that there was a connection.

Joseph expressed no recollection of our first meeting. I wasn't sure that he knew about Sharon and me. Perhaps he didn't want to know. Sharon had refused to talk much about Joseph. She had been attached to him in some manner she didn't want to explain. She always returned to him, yet she seemed to have no scruples about her infidelities. I might have been her last fling, but I wasn't her first.

Joseph didn't look good, giving credence to Frannie's claim that he was ill. He was thin, his skin sallow. He had that otherworldly look of someone close to death. Of course, I couldn't tell whether grief over Sharon was the cause of his rundown appearance. He was the high-strung type—the sort who carried everything to extremes.

Suddenly he sounded rational. "Listen," he said. "I know you spent a lot of time with Sharon. You might be in danger also."

"Why?"

"I don't know," he admitted. "I don't know exactly, but I think whoever did it was looking for something. Something that Sharon was hiding."

"What makes you think that?"

"This place was broken into a few days ago, but nothing was taken," he said with a strained look on his face, as if he were trying to remember something that happened a long time ago. "It was hard to tell that anyone had been in, but I could tell. I remember where everything is. If something is an inch from where I left it, I notice. This place had a thorough going over, all very neat, but also very thorough. Somebody was looking for something."

"Did you report it to the police?"

"Report what? Nothing was taken."

Ordinarily Joseph Hobart wasn't the sort of person who inspired a great deal of confidence, but for some reason, I began to see some glimmer of truth in what he was saying. Perhaps I didn't want to believe that Sharon's murder was a random act. Random happenings lack meaning and are short on dignity. Perhaps I wanted her death to assume significance beyond a crime statistic. Maybe Joseph wanted that also. I didn't know, but the seed was planted, and the only way I was going to have any peace was to satisfy myself about what really happened.

Joseph had calmed down considerably when his downstairs neighbor, Teri Shaunessy, knocked on the door. She came up to see how Joseph was doing. She was very solicitous. She was built like Sharon, but she was dark and there was more of her. She wore a tight pullover and overalls. Her breasts strained against the pullover. I stopped feeling sorry for Joseph. Frannie and I decided that Joseph was in good hands, and we didn't have to stick around any longer. I was glad to pass him on to someone else. I suppose Frannie was too.

It was dinner time; my stomach, neither patient nor subtle, began to growl. I persuaded Frannie to have a bite with me. We stopped off at the Ballroom. It was a nice restaurant in SoHo, and I always had a good time there, not just because of the food. The décor of the place soothed me. It had high ceilings, and there was a lot of green on the wall. Right then, I needed something to help me cope.

Stuart, the headwaiter, came over when he saw us. I was certain he remembered Frannie, although some time had passed since I had been there with her. Even I couldn't remember exactly when that had been, sometime before she had gone to California. I had been pissed about that too, among all the other things she did to annoy me. She had left when I needed her, and maybe I still resented that. Stuart greeted her as if we had been there only yesterday. He professed to remember her favorite table, and he led us straight to it.

The spark between Frannie and me was gone for the moment. It seemed strange to be with her and have no desire. I didn't know whether this neutral feeling had anything to do with Sharon's death or whether something else was going on. The restaurant was very relaxing. There was a piano player and a singer doing some show tunes. I got lost in the music for a while, but all the romantic songs reminded me of Sharon. I must have looked distressed because Frannie said, "Marc, you ought to take a vacation. Go out to the West Coast; visit your friends in San Francisco. It'll do you good." So, maybe she did have a good side. Maybe she was taking my feelings into account, and I should appreciate her effort. Or, maybe my distraught state had impaired my reasoning, and I was mistaking politeness for genuine concern, for affection perhaps. I had no choice but to enjoy the restaurant and trust her.

"I can't leave," I said. "There's something going on here and I intend to find out what. I owe it to Sharon. Maybe you can help me. How well did you know Charles Osgood?"

"Not well at all," she answered. The quality of her voice changed almost imperceptibly; some lines on her face tightened.

"I thought you might have known him since you and Sharon seemed to have so many friends in common."

"I stopped following Sharon's love affairs after a while. I don't mean to be indelicate; I know how you feel about her, but there were so many of them. All I know about Charles Osgood is that he used to work at Allied Chemicals. But he left the company awhile back."

"What did he do at Allied?"

"He was a department executive; I suppose in marketing or research or something or other; as I said, I didn't know him that well."

"But Larry must have known him."

"I suppose so," she answered without batting an eye. "He would have to, wouldn't he?"

"When Charles was killed you didn't discuss it?"

"He might have mentioned it in passing. We try to keep our professional lives out of our conversations."

"He would have to, wouldn't he?"

"As I said, Charles Osgood had already left the company."

"Ah, yes," I said. "And what do you make of all this, of Charles' death and now Sharon's?"

"You don't mean to say that you believe Joseph's ranting and raving? Crimes happen every day all around us. I don't see what connection there is between those two."

"Do you suppose all of this could be the machinations of a jealous husband?"

"Who, Joseph? Don't be absurd."

"Why is it absurd? The police think he might have killed Sharon."

"Why haven't they arrested him, then?"

"They have no case—just hunches."

"And what do you think? You think Joseph capable of such a thing?"

"Why not? He has the clearest motive."

"Why didn't he kill you then?"

"Maybe he wanted to; maybe he still does."

"Marco you can't believe that. Joseph wouldn't hurt a fly." She looked at me as if she had just discovered that I was a mad-bomber and a child molester. But her emotions were too much on the surface, a veneer on her face. I didn't know whether she was putting me on or whether she had succeeded in her quest for the ultimate cool, the inability to display sincerity. There was more to her than met the eye, but I couldn't tell what. I had to find out more about Charles, but Frannie was as unwilling to reveal anything about him as Sharon had been. It was useless to try to get anything else out of her.

"Well, Frannie," I said, "how are things between you and Larry?" I knew that would make her feel that I was still in love with her. A little flattery never hurts.

"They couldn't be better," she gloated.

"I suppose you'll be getting married soon," I said.

"I'm in no hurry," she said straining a little.

I decided to raise the ante just to make the game more interesting. "I'd like to get to know Larry a little before you two tie the knot. I don't want you and me to become strangers once you're married."

She extended both her hands across the table to rest them on my forearms, and with her sincerest expression of concern she said, "Marco, you haven't anything to fear. There'll always be a special place for you in my affection. Whatever happens, we'll always be friends."

She looked intently into my eyes, her chin thrust forward and her lips tightly pursed. Altogether, her pretty face reminded me of a very intense acorn. I was tempted to believe her words, but I had seen that expression too often to rely on it.

"We're entertaining a few people on the company yacht next weekend, Marco. Why don't you come along? You'll have a good time, and you'll have a chance to get acquainted with Larry. It'll be great if you come, please say yes."

"Frannie, you know I never can say no to you," I said.

After dinner we strolled through the SoHo streets. The city remained as noisy at night as it was in the daytime. But the night noise was somewhat different, like in the country where after dark the sounds of crickets replace everything else. Just as many people crowded the sidewalks at night as in the daytime, though maybe not the same people. The evening people are out to have a good time or to pretend they are having a good time. Sometimes they intend merely to fool their companions, but often they succeed in fooling themselves too, the city a willing accomplice in the deceit.

The shop windows suffused with light suggested a world where everything is special. The world of mannequins becomes the ideal. At first, under the intense display lights, it seems attractive enough, but soon you realize how bizarre it all looks. The streets of the city all lit up, perhaps circle downward to where, caught in a block of ice, a three headed figure in one mouth chews on Brutus, in the other on Cassius, and in the center, on Judas Iscariot.

I hailed a cab for Frannie, and then I walked home. I had a great deal to think about.

Chapter 9

WHEN I GOT HOME, there was a message from Romanelli on my answering machine, an apology for any unpleasantness he and his partner had caused me. He wanted to talk to me some more; would I go down to his office to see him?

The next day, I walked down 8th Street to St. Marks Place and across Tompkins Square Park. The precinct house was on Avenue C. In general, police stations are not the most pleasant environments. Romanelli's was no exception. Public buildings of each era tend to resemble each other. Why not? The likelihood was that the same bureaucrat was responsible for hiring the architect and the builder, the architect probably his wife's cousin and the contractor an old school chum.

The bottom of the edifice had that neo-Roman façade common to public structures of the early nineteen hundreds. Looking up beyond the first floor, you could tell from the units sticking out of the windows that the place had no central air-conditioning. I imagined Romanelli sitting at his desk sweating on hot summer days.

I introduced myself at the front desk. The officer sitting there gave me the once over, picked up the phone and said, "A Mr. Navarro to see you lieutenant." Then he turned to me and told me to take the stairs up to the second floor.

"Anywhere on the second floor?" I asked.

"Don't worry. Romanelli is hard to miss."

"That, I already know," I said and headed for the stairs.

At the top of the landing the first person I saw pointed to

an office across the room, and I proceeded in that direction. When I got to Romanelli's door, he was sitting at his desk—a metal job. He got up and extended his hand. He had a firm grip.

"Sit down," he said.

I sat on a vinyl-covered armchair.

"On second thought," he said, trying hard to win me over, "Why don't I buy you a drink. Everybody needs a lift now and then. There's a place around the corner."

We left the station and walked down the block. The storefront window at the bar hadn't been washed in some time, and the gold leaf that proclaimed it as Richie's Tavern was more than a little tarnished. We went in and sat at the bar. I was beginning to like Romanelli. There he sat in his gray nondescript suit, a delicate look about him. There was something desperate behind his eyes, a hunger rather. Not completely comfortable with himself, he knew there was something more to life than being a cop. He had glimpsed another kind of life, the kind he thought I had. I was that other kind of person about whom he knew little. Romanelli drank scotch; I drank bourbon.

Richie, the bartender proprietor, was a short man, the top of his head bald, hair only around his ears, his nose small, his mouth tight. He wore a white shirt and a black bow tie, his manner and dress made him seem out of place.

"Richie here was in the Merchant Marine," Romanelli said. "You should hear the stories. He's been in dives all over the world. You do any traveling Navarro? I've always wanted to travel myself, never had a chance."

"Not a traveling man either," I said.

"It's different when you have money. You go to the same place, but you see a different side of it."

"That's true," I said. "My grandfather was in the

Merchant Marine. During the war he was torpedoed twice. Hell of way to travel."

"Ship's Captain, your grandfather?"

"Cook's Mate."

"No kidding," Romanelli grunted incredulously. "What was he, the black sheep of the family?"

"On the contrary, he was the go-getter. Got to own a meat market…"

"What about your old man?"

I quaffed down what was left of my bourbon. I thought about the father I had invented. The image was tall and dark and had a very thin mustache. The eyes large, his hair receded from his forehead in undulating darkness. A white silk scarf trailed behind him in the breeze. A fog rolled in obscuring the landscape. Was it an airfield in which the ephemeral figure lived out his perfect life of adventure? I wasn't sure. I didn't know where I had picked up that image. The figure hung about in the darkness but clearly visible, like the protagonist on a darkened stage illuminated by a spotlight. The scene changes: the man wearing a trench coat brings his hand to his face to puff on a cigarette; then with a flick of the wrist he tosses it to the ground, and quickens his step as he spies a blond woman waiting under the awning at the corner store. She smiles on seeing him, her face lifts up to his. The image dissolves. I don't make out who the woman is. Sometimes I think it's my mother, but it's not always the same woman.

"My father died when I was a child," I said. "I don't even remember what he looked like. He was a salesman for a pharmaceutical company, traveled a great deal. He was killed in a plane crash."

Romanelli looked genuinely disturbed by that piece of information. "I'm sorry," he said. "It must've been rough growing up without a father."

"One manages," I said.

"Your mother remarried?"

"No, never. She was a young woman when it happened. But she pulled herself together and went out to work to support herself and me. Refused every suitor that came along. There were quite a few in the early years. She coped on her own until I was grown, and she's very proud of that. It was rough going, but we managed."

"Your life story is turning out to be quite different from what I imagined," Romanelli said. "I thought you grew up with money—private schools and all that."

"P. S. 99 in the Bronx," I informed him.

"One-o-seven, Brooklyn. Have another drink."

"Don't mind if I do."

"Ain't it a bitch how things always turn out to be different from what they seem? Seeing the way you live and who you hang out with, I was certain you were one of those effete snobs; know who I'm talking about? Money up the kazoo and never doing an honest day's work in their lives."

"I know who you mean," I said.

"But you're not one of those, are you?"

"No, I'm not," I assured him.

"She was a close friend of yours, wasn't she?"

I presumed he was referring to Sharon. "She certainly was," I said.

"We're gonna crack this case," he said. "I promise you."

"Okay," I said. "Now I'll buy you a drink."

Chapter 10

O N MY WAY HOME I reflected on what an okay guy Romanelli was turning out to be. In some ways he reminded me of Max, the doorman. When I had first moved into the building, on hearing my name, Max gave me a hard stare. He was very formal with me for a while, but I noticed that he was quite relaxed with everyone else, so I wondered whether unintentionally I had done something to turn him off. The last thing I wanted in a new place was to alienate the doorman. I reviewed all my interactions with him and I came up with nothing. I went out of my way to be nice to him and tried to figure out what was going on.

"How are you Max? Beautiful weather today," I said with a broad grin the next time I saw him.

"Yes sir," he said.

"You can skip the sir," I said. "Marc is good enough."

"Sure," he said, but doubt suffused his face. I was going to have to prove to him that I meant it. So I kept up my *bon hommerie*, and pretty soon I was getting more than I bargained for. Every time he saw me, he was ready to unburden. He droned on about his boxing career and how he had finally given it up, having succumbed to his childhood sweetheart who couldn't stand seeing him get banged around and getting home with a broken nose and a swollen face.

"So how does it feel being a married man?" I asked.

"It's okay," he said in a tone that implied that he had determined to refrain from negative comments. I figured I better not press him on it.

One day I got home just when he was going off duty, so I asked him where he lived. He said up in the Bronx.

"Well, that's my birthplace," I told him.

"No kidding," he said. He got even friendlier after that, until finally he asked me where my parents came from.

"They're from the Bronx too," I informed him. "But my grandparents came from Bayamon, Puerto Rico," I added.

That clinched it, and I figured I had made a friend for life. Of course, I saw behind his social façade some unexpressed question as to why and how I got to live on Fifth Avenue. I knew that eventually he would ask me, but he would wait for the right moment.

"You should take up boxing. I mean just as a hobby," Max once said to me. "It's good exercise for a guy, and it's kinda fun trying to knock somebody out."

I considered the other end of it, but after his shift one day, I went with Max down to a gym on the East Side, below Houston.

"Hey, Max, you brought a sparring partner today," said a scrawny looking guy sitting on a bench taking a rest after his workout.

"Oh, he's not ready for that yet," Max said to the perspiring squirt who smirked as if he understood something in Max's words that escaped me.

Every group has its particular signs and phrases that constitute its slang, and to be comfortable in the group, to be aware of what's being communicated, you have to learn the language. Entering a new turf can be somewhat disorienting. I walked into the place expecting it to be like the gym at the Y, but it wasn't. Even the smell in the air was different. Maybe boxers perspire a different substance than the rest of us. Possibly, but I decided to refrain from making a hasty judgment.

Anyway, Max introduced me to all the regulars at the

gym and to Agustin Rivera, an older guy, who ran the place. In his youth, he had attempted to break into boxing big-time, but as with everything else a great deal depended on luck, on being at the right place at the right time, and so the big time eluded him, but he had enjoyed doing what he did despite the lumps and the broken bones that went with it.

"So you want to box," Agustin said, looking me over as if to spot my weaknesses and possibly my strengths. What the total balance was, he didn't tell me and I didn't ask. I figured I'd just go along and maybe enjoy the experience, though I wasn't looking forward to having my face pounded. I recalled my first fight in the street when I was a kid and how surprised I was at how a punch to the face really felt. I had gotten used to seeing movie and television figures punch each other out, even break chairs on each other's heads, and still enjoy it. Imagine my astounding discovery that the activity was more painful than thrilling.

"It's an art," Agustin said. "When you do it right, you feel connected to the world. It adds meaning to your life."

"Is that what it is?" I said thinking that there had to be a better way to arrive at the meaning of life without acquiring the black and blue lumps, but maybe I was wrong, and these guys who went about punching each other unconscious had discovered something that escaped philosophers sitting at their desks ruminating about existence.

Back in the gym, after I changed into a t-shirt and sweatpants for the workout, Agustin said to me, "Let's see what you can do. You look pretty fit for a beginner."

"Oh, I work out every morning," I said. "The ladies like a healthy looking guy."

"So they do," Agustin said with a straight face, "and they don't mind a bump here and there."

Max had lent me boxing gloves, an extra pair he carried around in his gym bag. Agustin examined them.

"These will do for the time being," he said. "Let me see you punch the bag."

Boxing was far from my favorite sport; still, I got into the habit of going down to the gym to spar with Max. There was something satisfying about hanging out in a grungy environment. You might say I was slumming, but that's not it at all. There was some part of me that belonged there, and I knew it. A lot of the guys who worked out at the gym were struggling to put food on the table, but maybe they weren't all that different from me. You know the saying, "There but for the grace of God..." So Max and his buddies still lived in the Bronx while I had a Fifth Avenue address down in the Village. I tried to keep that in the background, but Max didn't seem to notice my attempt. For him, my address was a badge I should wear proudly.

"He grew up in the South Bronx," Max was fond of pointing out to his friends at the gym, "but now he lives on Fifth Avenue."

"You mean up in Harlem?"

"Shit, man, don't get wise with me. I mean right down by Washington Square," Max retorted.

"Hey guys," I said, "let's stick to the workout, and leave real estate out of it."

One day a couple of guys came down to the gym looking for Max, but they didn't say so right away. Agustin went over to them and asked if they wanted a tour of the place. For a second, they wondered whether he was kidding.

Then the taller of the two said, "Sure, show us around, looks like an interesting place."

This guy had a belly that stuck out, probably sliding over the buckle of his belt, but I couldn't ascertain that because he was wearing a two-button sports jacket that was too small on him, and he kept it buttoned at both places, like no one had ever informed him of how uncool that was. His shirt collar splayed over the jacket collar, something I hadn't seen anyone do for ages.

I wondered whether he had jell in his hair, but I figured asking him on first encounter might be considered impolite. The second guy was short and thin, and his jacket was too big on him. Maybe they had bought them at the same time, two same size jackets for the price of one.

The tall guy turned to the short one and said, "We do want to look around, don't we, Pablo?"

"So what's your name," Agustin asked, "or are you both called Pablo?"

"What are you, a wise guy?" the tall guy said still refraining from revealing his name. "He's a wise guy, isn't he?" he said to his partner.

"He sure is," Pablo said.

"Hey, your name is your name," Agustin said. "You can keep it a secret if you want. It's all the same to me."

"See, he's obliging," the tall guy said to Pablo.

"He sure is," Pablo retorted.

By that time I was ready to demonstrate a punch to the plexus, but I was having one of my humble days, so I held back figuring that Agustin was used to dealing with tough guys and probably had a better technique than I did. I could watch Agustin and learn something.

"I could show you the door," Agustin said.

"Don't get antsy," the tall one said. "We know where the door is. Don't we Pablo?"

"We sure do," Pablo said.

"Then you know it's a short walk to it."

"You gonna show us the place or not?" the tall one continued.

"I think you've seen enough of it," Agustin said.

"Now, you see, you've lost your cool. That ain't nice. I thought this was a friendly place."

At that point, Agustin kept quiet. He had said enough as far as he was concerned. He figured the guys were a couple of pranksters. The pressures of city life had been too much for them, and they had snapped. One was bound to run into that type sooner or later.

"We are not interested in the place anyway," the tall one said.

Agustin stared first at one then at the other. These were nut jobs for sure. He turned his back on them and started towards his office.

"We're looking for Max," the tall one said. "Is he around?"

Agustin stopped and turned to face the two strangers again. "He ain't been around today," Agustin said.

"Well maybe we'll hang out here for a while and wait for him."

"You do that if you want to, but he usually doesn't show up this late."

"That's all right. We have some time to spare."

"What do you want with Max, anyway?" Agustin asked.

"What is it to you? We're here on private business."

"This ain't a private place," Agustin informed him.

"Is that so?" the tall guy said. "You want my mother's maiden name?"

"Only if she wants to join the club," Agustin said.

"So you cater to female boxers, do you?"

"I don't cater to nobody," Agustin said.

"So you're a tough guy, are you?"

"I'm tough enough," Agustin said. "In case you haven't noticed."

"Well, well, well, I wouldn't wanna mess with you."

"So long as we understand each other," Agustin continued.

"We're just here on business," the tall guy said.

"Oh yeah, so what kind of business are you in?"

"It's got nothing to do with you."

"I'm just curious," Agustin said. "I don't like other business transpiring in my place."

"If you must know, we're bill collectors," the tall one said.

"Is that so?"

"Isn't that so?" the tall guy said turning to his partner.

"Looks that way to me," his partner replied.

"Well, I don't owe anything, and I won't have you collecting from anyone in here."

"Don't worry," the tall one said. "We'll collect from Max outside."

"Make sure you stick to that," Agustin said.

Agustin turned again to walk away from the two strangers. I had been standing by the punching bag listening to them. Agustin looked straight at me as if he wanted to tell me something. I figured he was suggesting I go out and look for Max and warn him in case he was on his way to the place. I had left my phone in the locker. I could go to the locker room and try to call Max, but he had no cell phone. If he was on the way already, I wouldn't reach him. I could go down to the street and wait for him there, but of course I didn't know whether he was on his way or not.

I went down to the locker room and dialed his home number. I let it ring a long time; still, there was no answer. I skipped the shower, got dressed, and went down to the street. I waited out front for a while until I got anxious about the possibility that the bozos would come down and ask me why I was still there. I crossed the street to the coffee shop and ordered a cup, and through the storefront I kept my eye on the street. If I saw Max, I would stop him before he got to the gym, but I didn't think he was going to show up that late anyway.

I had to find Max and tell him about these guys in case he didn't yet know they were looking for him. Probably he already knew they were after him, and that's why he hadn't shown up at the gym. Probably he wasn't home either, since those guys must have known his address and would eventually go there looking for him. But maybe they had decided to put the gym ahead, since that was his routine at that time of day. Anyway, I needed a first stop, and his place topped the list. Actually, so far it was the only item on the list.

I rode up to the Bronx. He had an apartment in a five-story building, the kind built in the late forties after the war. I rang the bell downstairs and got no answer. Either there was nobody home or whoever was there had decided to play dead. Hoping that Max would somehow guess that it was me, I kept ringing for a while.

There was no response, but a kid opened the door on his way out, and I slipped in before the door banged close and locked again. I walked up to apartment 3B and put my ear to the door. I heard nothing. Maybe there was no one home after all. I knocked and waited for a response. No one came to the door; then I thought I heard some shuffle inside. I knocked again.

"Hello in there! This is Marco Navarro," I said loud enough for anyone inside to hear me. "Max are you in there?"

I heard some steps inside, someone gingerly walking up to door, probably to peek through the peephole.

"I'm looking for Max. I'm a friend of his," I said.

"Max ain't here," a woman voice came through.

I put on the friendliest tone I could muster. "I need to talk to him. Please tell me where I can find him."

Of course, I've been told several times that voice control isn't my forte. But maybe I was getting better at it, because the woman continued in a more relaxed tone. "Who did you say you are?" she inquired.

"I'm a friend of Max's. I live in the building where he works."

There was a long silence. Then I heard the lock click and the door opened slightly partially revealing the tense face of a young woman. I smiled trying to reassure her.

"Hi," I said. "Really, I need to speak to Max. Do you know where he is?"

She looked straight at my face. She must have been looking for a sign that would assure her that she could trust me. Generally, I'm pretty sure of my facial ability to confirm my honesty, but for a moment there, I thought it was failing. She looked down at my feet, and maybe I was wearing the right kind of shoes, because after that, she opened the door wide enough for me to walk in.

I entered the dimly lit hallway and she closed the door behind us. Under my feet worn linoleum pretended to be wood. The smell of Latin cooking in the air reminded me of my mother. I had to go down to see her pretty soon, before she began to think of me as a negligent son. At the moment, I had to deal with a more pressing problem. I had to figure out how much trouble Max was in. I asked the young woman for Max's whereabouts.

"He's not here," she tentatively said. "Can you help him?" she asked me.

"I first have to know what's going on," I said.

"I'll tell you where he is," she said, "if you promise to help him."

"Just tell me," I said. "I'll see what I can do."

The apartment reminded me of my childhood. The cheap upholstered furniture had plastic covers, a look I had grown to hate. I couldn't understand the logic. It was as if merely having food in the house would sustain you without eating it.

"He's over at his uncle's place," she said, "up on Kelly Street."

She picked up the phone and called the uncle to tell him I was on my way. When I got there a woman opened the door. I figured she was Max's aunt, but no, I later found out she was the uncle's third wife or rather third woman. Max's aunt had been the second.

"Down that way," the woman said pointing down the corridor. She stepped back into the kitchen, and I proceeded down the hallway. A man emerged from one of the doorways, and I presumed he was the uncle. This time I was right. Don Pedro beckoned me as he said, "He's down this way, in the bedroom."

I followed Don Pedro to the next door, where he pointed to Max lying on the bed in a semi-curled up almost fetal position and facing the wall.

"Is he all right?" I asked Don Pedro.

He shrugged his shoulder. I proceeded to the side of the bed and said, "Max, it's me, Marco. Talk to me."

He turned around and stared at me, but he didn't say anything.

"What's going on?"

"They're after me," he said.

"I know, but why?"

"I owe some money."

"That's simple enough to fix," I said. "I'll give you the money."

"It's too late," he said.

"Nah," I tried to reassure him, "a little more interest, that's all."

"No, you don't understand. They want to make an example out of me. They're like that, crazy guys."

"Profit is profit," I said. "I'm sure they'd rather make money than not."

"You're reasonable, but they're different. You don't know these people. You live in another world."

"Nah," I said, "the world is all the same. Money talks." I wasn't sure whether I was right this time.

"Thanks for coming over," Max said, "but I don't want you getting in trouble. One target is enough."

"One is too many," I said. "Tell me where I can find these people, and I'll work out a deal."

"Save yourself," Max said and again turned his face to the wall.

There was nothing else I could say to him. I had to proceed on my own. While I spoke to Max, his uncle had stood by the door. I looked at him hoping for some clue. I suppose he guessed what I wanted.

"You think you can handle this?" he asked.

"I can try," I said. "Can you get me in touch with these guys?"

"Sure," he said, "but do you really want to get involved?"

"Don't you want to help your nephew?"

I guess he did, because he signaled me to follow him into the living room. I figured I could just offer to pay Max's debt, and I saw no reason why they would refuse the deal. Don Pedro made some phone calls and got an address, and I proceeded there thinking the problem would be simply resolved. I walked up from Kelly Street to Southern Boulevard and down towards Hunt's Point, to a building that had once housed a Lowes theater.

I took the steps up to the second floor and searched the hallway for the Hunts Point Social Club. When I found a door so labeled, I paused for a second, then I turned the doorknob and to my surprise it wasn't locked. I walked in to see Pablo Nieves and Tuto Rodriguez, the two bill collectors, engaged in a game of pool on a child size pool table.

"So what do you know," Tuto said. "If it isn't an old acquaintance."

Pedro, leaning over the table to take a shot, looked up and smirked, but kept his mouth shut.

"So which way to the man?" I asked.

"Are you here on business?"

"I didn't come to play pool," I said.

"How much?"

"I thought you were the collector not the lending agent."

"It depends on the time of day," he said.

"I'm here to close Max's account."

"Is that so?"

"Would I lie to you?"

"We only deal with the principal."

"Isn't that called cash?"

"That all depends."

"I'd like to talk to the boss."

"Well, you're talking to him."

"I don't think so."

"Thinking gets you in trouble."

"Or visa-versa."

"You mean trouble can get you thinking?"

"You're smarter than you look."

"You're a wise guy."

"I'm glad you noticed."

The door at the end of the room opened to reveal a short heavyset guy in a white shirt but no tie; suspenders held up his pants. I figured he was the guy I was looking for. He had the face of cherub, but I knew that was an illusion. You might say that's common enough; we all have our dark side. Except, this guy probably didn't have anything else, or so I concluded on first glimpse of Mundo Gonzales.

"He's here about Max," Tuto said.

The short fat guy reached for the knob, I presumed he was going to shut the door on me.

"You throw away money?" I asked.

He held the doorknob trying to decide whether to proceed with shutting me out or listening to what I had to say. He must have been having a boring day and figured I could entertain him with a harebrained scheme. He tilted his head signaling me to step in. His waist too wide for me to slip by him, I waited for him to move aside. He turned and walked into the room and I followed. He sat at an old wooden office desk that had seen its day at the Salvation Army. The light green walls of the room were completely bare and initially disconcerted me. What did I expect, pictures of his wife and children? I waited for him to say something, but he just sat there staring at me.

Finally I said, "I'm ready to make good on Max's debt."

"Are you?"

Was there more here than Max had told me? It seemed as if more than an exchange of dollars was required.

"He owes you a sum that I'm willing to provide. Am I missing something here?"

"He's taken too long. I have to make an example out of him."

"A late fee, I understand."

"Yes, a late fee," he said, "but not in dollars."

"Let's be reasonable."

"He'll survive."

"That's not the point."

"The point is that I can't put that much effort into trying to collect, you know what I mean? If I let him off lightly, everyone else will think they can get away with it. You understand, don't you? This is just business, nothing else."

"Well, let's be creative about this. There's got to be another way of solving the problem."

"Okay, you tell me," he said.

I was ready to tell him that his ears were not exactly the most salient part of his body, but I restrained myself. After all, we were still talking, so maybe the guy had a reasonable side. Wonders never cease.

"We can fake it," I said. "I'll have him bandaged up and advertise it as Tuto's handiwork. That'll do it, if publicity is what you're after." Of course, hearing my own words I was proud of myself. I thought it was a great idea and on top of that humorous.

"I don't think so," Mundo said. "It's been done before. I've seen that on TV. You picked it up from one of those cop shows, didn't you?"

"I'm being original here," I said. Actually, I thought I was, but Mundo wasn't buying it.

"I'll tell you what," he said. "I like you, so I'll give you until tomorrow to come up with something."

"Thanks," I said. "You're all right."

"What about the mullah? I'll take that now."

"I didn't come exactly loaded," I said. "Just tell me the exact amount, and I'll have it the next time I see you."

"Tuto will tell you on your way out."

After talking with Tuto, I walked down the stair to find myself again on Southern Boulevard.

Chapter 11

I HAD TO COME up with a solution to Max's problem, but the questions prompted by Sharon's death still hovered over me. I thought back to the day after Charles was killed—the day after Sharon and I spent the night together for the first time. I had been curious about Charles, but she wasn't about to give me any satisfactory answers. After breakfast at Feathers, we had walked about the Village. The sky unusually blue for New York, the air crisp, we felt good walking around. We strolled down Bleecker Street looking in the shop windows. She loved antiques. They had no fascination for me, but I didn't let on. I was just happy to be with her. She hung on to my arm.

"I'm really curious about you," she said.

"And I about you," I retorted.

"There's nothing mysterious about me," she protested. "I'm a plain ordinary woman. You on the other hand are an enigma."

"How so?"

"You haven't explained to me how you maintain your life style. How do you earn a living?"

"It's all very simple," I said. "I'm lucky at playing the market."

"You always had money?"

"I grew up in the Bronx. My father was killed in an accident. My mother had to go out and work. I was shuttled from aunt to aunt, the day-care centers of those days. I was the stickball champion of Kelly Street—a two-sewer man, three with the wind behind me. How's that for a portrait of a Wall Street hustler?"

"How did you get started?"

"All I ever wanted was to write. But I never had time, you know. I always had to work. Since I was fourteen years old I worked. I delivered groceries after school; I shined shoes; I sold papers. All through college I worked, summers too. All those jobs! That's a story in itself. At the university, I got into writing. But I still had to earn a living. For a while I got along with very little, working only part-time. But I was really living from hand to mouth. I wasn't doing the kind of writing that would make it all seem worthwhile, and I was feeling guilty as hell that my mother was still working. To top it all I got married. My wife just wasn't cut out for the down and out way of life; at least, she wasn't then. She's changed somewhat since those days."

"Ah, yes, tell me about your wife. What was she like? I'm dying of curiosity."

"No, not today," I said. "Let's not ruin the day."

"A bitter divorce?"

"No, actually it was quite amicable as far as those things go, and we're still friends, but my marriage was not the most pleasant episode of my life."

"And what was the most pleasant episode of your life?" she asked.

"I'm living through it right now."

"Oh, I see."

"Shortly after my divorce, I got a very pleasant surprise. Like out of a storybook, an inheritance from my Aunt Petrina. It wasn't all that much, as money goes, but it was enough to get me started. God bless Aunt Petrina. She was a funny old lady. When she was alive, I didn't think she liked me, then she left me all that money. She was my father's sister. The strange part was that she never lifted a finger to help my mother and me after his death. My mother, however, is a very proper woman, and we always kept in touch with

Petrina. We invited her to our little family parties. We called her on her birthday and so on. But she always seemed indifferent to our attention."

"Were you nice to her because she was wealthy?"

"Wealthy? We hadn't the slightest idea. She lived like a pauper."

"Oh, there must be more to her. Weren't you ever curious to find out what she was really like? I mean, after she left you the money?"

"All I know is that she didn't get along with most people, least of all her own family. Of course, I don't know how she related to my father. She had another brother, Uncle Luis, and they couldn't stand each other. He's not the greatest guy either. Ever since I got Aunt Petrina's money, he hasn't spoken to me. He feels he and his children are entitled to at least some of it, if not all."

"Are they?"

"She left it to me, and I'm not giving it away. I think I earned it. It wasn't easy being nice to Aunt Petrina, even when she wasn't being totally obnoxious. There were times when she made my life rather miserable. I remember her being sick once, and she wanted somebody to read to her. My mother made me go there and keep Aunt Petrina company. It was torture for me. Her apartment had a very musty feel. It was small, and everything was pushed up against the moss green walls, where a multitude of cheap prints resembled crawling objects. Propped up in bed on a pile of very lacy pillows, she had two of her cats in the bed with her; the other two roamed around the room. I hated those cats, especially when I went to the bathroom, and there was a box of kitty litter that hadn't been changed for days. So, there I was with the musty odor, a claustrophobic feeling, the hateful cats and a crotchety old lady who wanted me to read *Nicholas Nickleby* to her. You can't imagine how boring that book can be to a ten year old boy."

"I can imagine," she said. "But you got your reward."

"I earned every penny of it," I said, although I didn't always feel that way. "I'm the best thing that could have happened to that money. I made it grow."

"So you became a speculator instead of a writer."

"I became a speculator to become a writer."

"Oh, I see. Does that really work?"

She had that mischievous look again. Her poking fun at me made me uneasy, shook me up, but I guess it didn't shake me enough to make me defensive. She knew just how far to go. I didn't want to talk about me. I wanted to find out about Charles and about Joseph.

"Won't Joseph be wondering where you are?" I asked.

"Changing the subject, are you?"

"You've had your twenty questions. Now I'll have mine."

"He's away," she said. "He's often away. We give each other space."

"And you don't ask him what he does while he's away, and he doesn't ask you."

"That's right," she said.

"What was that little episode at the Thompson party then?"

"That was something else altogether. He mistook you for someone else."

"For Charles?"

"Maybe."

"You're not going to tell me."

"No, I'm not. Let's take a ride on the Staten Island Ferry," she suggested putting her nose up to mine and wrapping her arms around me.

She played the game better than I, but I was learning fast. Her kiss gave me a funny sensation behind my ear, like having too many sweets or too much vinegar. We walked to the Sheridan Square subway stop. Before we went through the turnstile, I noticed a man talking on his cell phone. He looked familiar, but I couldn't place him.

"You see that man over there," I said to Sharon, "have you seen him before?"

"Sure," she answered, "I saw him a few minutes ago on Greenwich Avenue."

"But not before that?"

"Not that I recall."

"Maybe he was at the disco last night."

"Maybe he was. I don't know."

"This is too much of a coincidence. Why would anybody want to follow you?"

"If you don't know by now, I can't help you," she said grinning.

"I'm serious. Would Joseph have you followed?"

"Don't be ridiculous."

"There something you're not telling me."

"Please, don't spoil the day," she implored sounding desolate.

"Last night a man you knew was killed while being pursued by strangers, and you didn't want to stay to give the police a statement. And now, we are being followed. I can't imagine why anybody would want to follow me, so they must be following you. Don't you think you better tell me what's going on?"

"Marco, I would tell you, if I knew. Believe me I'm as much in the dark about this as you are."

"Tell me about Charles."

"You don't really want to know about Charles."

"Yes, I do."

"He wasn't a very nice person. I had something with him, but it was over. He wanted me back—very unreasonable man. Last night he wanted me to go with him right then. He's crazy."

"Why did you start up with a man like that anyway?"

"I didn't know he was going to turn out so unpleasant. He seemed at first attractive. There was something unpredictable about him that excited me."

"I see."

"Now you're upset."

"I'm not upset," I said. I was jealous of a dead man. "Why was he killed?"

"Why is anybody killed in a traffic accident?"

"Was it an accident?"

She looked annoyed and didn't answer. I would ruin the day if I kept questioning her. That certainly wasn't what I wanted. The man by the phone might be just a coincidence. Out of jealousy no doubt, I was blowing things out of proportion. What the hell, Charles was dead. I didn't have to worry about him anymore. For some reason, I wasn't jealous of Joseph. Husbands are never a problem in that respect, perhaps because they are the losers. They have been left. One feels superior to them. Other men, however, became the threat. If a woman is unfaithful to her husband, why wouldn't she be unfaithful to her lover? Every man she looks at becomes a potential competitor. Charles was dead, but it bothered me that she had been attracted to someone who seemed so different from me.

When we got on the subway, the man was still by the turnstile. Maybe he wasn't following us after all. We sat down. The subway car was very bright, the cars narrower and shorter than on most other routes, the light more concentrated. I felt constricted, and more than glad to get out at South Ferry leaving behind the oppressive feeling of confinement. When we got to the dock, a boat had just left.

The atmosphere in the terminal was very different from the subway, the opposite actually. There's a lot of space, high ceilings at the entrance, suitable preparation for going out on the bay, although the place looked typically grimy on a Saturday afternoon. I searched around for misplaced characters, a useless endeavor. No one ever looks out of place at a terminal. Anyway, I had convinced myself to put away my paranoia and enjoy my day with Sharon. We waited twenty minutes for the next boat.

When it arrived, we moved to the entrance gate and waited for the passengers to disembark. A slight breeze wafted in from the bay. An attendant drew back the spring barrier and signaled for waiting passengers to board. The texture of the flooring changed from cement to steel and on the boat to wood. The mooring released, at the seaside end the propeller churned the water producing a guttural sound. We moved out into the bay, and in a little while the outline of the city dwarfed in the distance. The dark water stretched out ahead of us. The seagulls squawked and dived for their meal. Above, the silver clouds rolled into grand shapes, festive and ebullient. I resolved to stay sunny. I kept my eyes on Sharon.

"I love this," she said as she looked out at the brilliant sky. "And I love being here with you."

That's all I needed to hear. I was ready to believe whatever story she might tell me about anything. On the ferry, the whole world became simple: the sky, the wind, the water, and the boat. There was nothing else. I was filled with a bittersweet anxiety that the intimacy wouldn't last, that it wasn't even real. I had occasionally felt close to other women, but Sharon was different. Maybe I had been alone for too long, had too many dinners by myself, had too often awakened in an unfamiliar bedroom with someone I hoped I wouldn't have to see again, feeling guilty that I felt that way, as if I didn't know that my partner felt the same.

I wanted Sharon never to go away, and I was frightened when I imagined her absence. After all, she was married, and she had not expressed any intention of changing that. I was being my perverse self—wanting what was most difficult if not impossible to get. I had her for the moment, and the moment should have been enough, but I feared that it was coming to an end. It wasn't even that I wanted her to live with me, although it would come down to that, in practical terms. What I wanted was for her to love me, or rather, for me to feel that she loved me absolutely. To get rid of the painful anxiety, I needed an opiate, and I tried to drug myself on her physical attributes. I tried to drown my senses in hers. I was happy, but not for long. Out of the corner of an eye, I glimpsed a familiar figure.

"Hey, there's that fellow again. This time I'm going to find out what he wants."

"Don't, Marco, don't look for trouble. You'll get hurt. This has nothing to do with you."

"I'm going to find out once and for all. You stay put."

I moved into the cabin. Our friend was sitting on one of the benches in the middle. He got up when he saw me. I lost sight of him for a minute as he ducked into the stairway in the center housing. He must have descended to the auto deck. I followed. I saw the familiar jacket down towards the bow. Facing away from me, he pretended to be getting into his car. I made my way down along the side, then around the autos. I was working myself up anticipating that he would give me a hard time. I wondered whether he was armed. He was either very sure that he could handle me, or he was very inept at his job. He was average height, but he had bulk. His face wide, rather flat, his nose had been broken more than once.

"You want something from me?" I asked in a calm but deliberate voice.

"I beg your pardon?" he said, feigning surprise.

"You've been following me all day. I want to know why."

I stood close enough to let him know I meant business, and also not to give him enough room to maneuver. But I had not expected him to take this tack. The thought suddenly struck me that I might be acting very imprudently. However, when you can't retreat, the best defense is to advance. Grabbing the lapels of his jacket, I banged him against the car.

"What are you crazy or something?" he shouted.

"Who hired you?"

"I don't know what you're talking about. If this is a mugging you're not going to get away with it."

"Who hired you to follow me?"

"I'm not following you. I never saw you before in my life."

"You got some ID?"

He made a move for his inside pocket, but I stopped him, not knowing what he'd pull out. I reached for his ID, but before I could look at it, I felt a sharp sting at the back of my head. The boat suddenly became unstable, as if it were tipping to one side. My knees gave way and everything blacked out. The next moment, I became aware of faces staring down at me. Some of them seemed concerned, Sharon kneeling beside me, her eyes moist.

"Oh, Marco," she said when my eyes opened.

With a dull pulsating pain, my head felt like it had grown to ten times its normal size. As I tried to get up, I noticed blood on the ground beside me. It took me a few seconds to realize it was my own.

"Marco, what happened?"

"He had a partner," I said.

"You have a nasty cut on your head. You might need stitches. We better get you some help."

"I've stopped bleeding, haven't I?"

"Yes, but you can't just let it go."

"That's an ugly gash," a bystander said. There were a few grunts of assent.

The ferry was slowing down; the engine had gone into

reverse. I was going to miss the docking. That was always the most exciting part of the trip. Obviously, the incident had not yet been reported to anyone in the crew, and I preferred it that way. Otherwise, the boat would be taken out of service until the police arrived, and no one would be let off, interfering with everyone's plans for the day including my own. Besides, I would only be able to identify one of the guys, and he would claim that I assaulted him and he defended himself. I decided not to involve the police. Maybe that was a mistake, but just then it seemed like a good idea.

The thought of going to a hospital really made me feel ill. A person could die in a New York hospital from a minor cut. "No, hospital," I said. "I'll have my own doctor look at it."

"All right," Sharon said, "right now." She took charge very naturally, like a mother. She was a bundle of contradictions. I thought I could get to like that. She volunteered to call the doctor.

"I can call him myself," I said. "I'm not so hurt I can't talk."

"That's for sure."

I retrieved my phone, called and got the service. "I want to talk to Dr. Feldman, I said. This is Marco Navarro, it's an emergency." I said that mostly for Sharon's benefit. The service didn't know who I was, and even if it did, the person on the phone wouldn't have cared. "I have to speak to the doctor right away. Can he call me back within the next ten minutes?"

"We'll do our best to reach him."

"Please do," I said. I gave them my number and hung up. Five minutes later my phone rang. "Hello Sid, how are you?"

"I'm fine," he said, "but you didn't call just to inquire after my health I'll bet."

I told him about the gash in my head.

"Come right up," he said.

"I'm still in Staten Island."

"I wouldn't invest in Staten Island real estate," he said.

"Things are changing," I said.

"Really? What the hell are you doing out there?"

"I'll tell you when I see you," I said

To avoid the crowd, we waited to get off. Sharon seemed very nervous. Suddenly, the possibility that I had been searched, while unconscious, dawned on me. I check my pockets to see if anything had been taken. I had everything. It wasn't a robbery, or at least, they didn't take anything I was aware of having.

We took the next boat back and a taxi to Sid's place on Barrow Street. He answered the door. He was my ex-wife's uncle. I had known him longer than I had known her. In fact, I met her at his office. She was working there as his receptionist for a while, part-time after school. We were still college students back then. Sid and I had met while skiing. Hurtling down the mountain, I hit a patch of ice, slid out of control, my foot coming to rest up against a boulder. I thought I had broken some bones, but luckily I had only a sprained ankle. Sid just happened to be coming down behind me. He stayed with me till the ski patrol arrived, and he went down with us, bandaged up my foot.

He was my kind of doctor, plain, unpretentious, and friendly. Off the ski slope, he had a gray mousy appearance, but that proved deceiving—an affectation of dress and manner. Underneath the drab appearance lurked a sparkling sense of humor and a devilish wit. A very kindly man, he still didn't understand what had gone wrong with my marriage to Gail.

Sid didn't have regular office hours on Saturdays. He came to the door in an old sweatshirt and jeans. He had been working in his garden. His face lit up when he saw Sharon, and he frowned when he turned to me.

"Let's look at you," he said in the tone of voice that precedes a lecture. "I didn't think street brawling was exactly your style," he continued.

"It wasn't exactly a brawl," I said.

He looked at me skeptically. I introduced Sharon, and we all proceeded into the examination room. I sat down on a stool, and Sid poked around the back of my head.

"It's nothing," he said. "You don't even need stitches."

He cleaned the wound with something that stung like the dickens. Then he bandaged me up. I looked like an extra for *The Red Badge of Courage.* I could tell that Sid wanted to ask me more questions about the incident, but he didn't want to do it in front of Sharon.

"Let's go upstairs and have a drink," he said. "You can explain to me what you were doing on Staten Island to provoke such a vicious attack."

"We were just being romantic," she said. "That's all."

"Sometimes that's enough," he said, darting a furtive glance at me. He had noticed her wedding ring. Later on, when Sharon had excused herself and gone in search of the bathroom, he tapped my head and said, "That's what comes of running around with other men's wives."

He was possibly right. He knew whereof he spoke. He had done plenty of running around himself in his day. The good doctor asked us to stay for dinner, but we declined. I was tired. Home was the most inviting place at the moment. It was a nice walk through the more quiet streets of the Village, though the ambiance began to change as we proceeded down West 4th to Washington Square. The park was back to being sort of scruffy after having been renovated to erase the ambiance it had acquired in the sixties as an exhibit place for the counterculture, or so I had heard from the older folk. Anyway, I was used to the park's grunginess, but I imagined what it must have been like back then when the young attempted to drop the traditional and go for the ideal. Those times were gone, but maybe they would come around again. My mother said that to me once. She was sorry I had missed that era.

When we got to my place, Sharon said she had to leave. She wanted to be home before Joseph returned. I wasn't disappointed enough to argue with her. I needed to be alone to mull things over. A lot had happened in the previous twenty-four hours.

She got ready to go. "Don't forget your change of clothes," I said.

"No chance," she said. "I left everything on the bed."

She went into the bedroom to fetch her wares.

"They're not here," she said.

I followed her in and looked around. Her clothes were not in the bedroom. We went back into the living room.

"Ah, here they are," I said. Her belongings lay on one of the chairs.

"I must have moved everything this morning and forgot all about it," she said. She stared at me for a minute then started to say goodbye.

"Must you leave?"

"I have to," she said.

I accompanied her down to the street, and after kissing her goodbye, I watched her walk down Fifth Avenue into Washington Square.

Chapter 12

SHARON'S CONNECTION TO corporate people went back to her family. Although she was an actress married to a sculptor, she came from a whole other world, one on which she heaped a great deal of scorn. Still, she seemed unable to stay away from it. Her father had been a manufacturer of industrial machinery. He had built his business from the ground up, and he knew every inch of every plant he owned. He was an industrialist of the old school. Of course, the old school was long gone, but he was still around and out of sync with the times.

Sharon's maiden name was Winkler. Her father, Mathew Winkler, was a rotund man who liked to compare himself to Winston Churchill. For some reason, no longer remembered, his friends called him Toby. I saw him only once while Sharon was alive, and I could tell right off that he detested me. He couldn't stand to lose anything. Not only had Hobart taken his little girl away from him (She had thrown herself away on a fellow who wasn't man enough to keep her), but now she flaunted a lover. At least Hobart was legal, me I didn't have a leg to stand on. I presumed he didn't know about the others.

I hadn't been planning to meet Sharon's family when I agreed to drive up to Massachusetts for a weekend. We were just going for a drive and a stopover at Tanglewood to take in some music. She convinced me to take a side road, so we could enjoy the Berkshire scenery.

"Turn in on the next driveway," she said.

A formal entrance suddenly loomed, brick side pillars

and fancy iron gates. They were open. We turned onto a road that proceeded through some lush greenery that gave the impression of natural conservation, but I had a feeling it received high maintenance. In less than a mile, the forest cleared on one side to reveal a lake. In the distance, on the lake side of the road, a house appeared.

"I guess we're visiting someone."

"We certainly are," she said.

"Don't do this to me, Sharon," I said. I had a definite premonition that I wasn't going to enjoy this little side trip.

"It won't be bad," she said. "It's only my mom and dad."

"Oh, Jesus Christ, Sharon, we can't do this."

"Well, we're here already and they saw us. My mom is by the window."

We proceeded up the gravel driveway to the house. I glanced up and noticed the gables. I didn't count, but probably there were more than seven. The roof, a prevalent dark gray announcing New England, hovered above the pristine white walls. Suddenly, a dog emerged ferociously barking at the car.

"What's the matter with that dog? It never saw a BMW before?"

"Please relax, everything is going to be all right." She stepped out of the car. "Be quiet Queenie," she commanded. The dog immediately shut up.

Mrs. Winkler met us at the door. She didn't have the look I expected of Sharon's mother. That is to say, she wasn't much like Sharon. Mrs. Winkler, a wispy woman, whose face gave the impression of high maintenance, at moments, had a luminescent quality that gave way to the scrubbed look often seen on the faces of nuns. Parsimonious with her movements, she appeared to arrive at places without moving her feet. Her eyes, a pale gray variety, verged on coldness so unremarkable as to render that designation too strong.

Sharon bent over to kiss her mother. The daughter enveloped the older woman in a frightening voluptuousness from which the mother instinctively recoiled. The action was ever so slight, the mother catching herself in mid-act and forcing herself to submit to affection that her intellect told her was natural. Sharon seemed unperturbed by the exchange. The walls seemed to withdraw before the force of her presence.

"Darling, I'm so glad to see you," Mrs. Winkler said. Her gray eyes glazed with moisture.

"This is my friend, Marco Navarro," Sharon said turning to me.

"How do you, Mr. Navarro?" Mrs. Winkler said and dutifully extended her hand.

With a trace of sensuousness, her fingers seemed to dissolve in mine, an allusion to either a forgotten actuality or a suppressed potential. Bewildered by having to relate to a stranger, she turned again to her daughter.

"Your father is out back. I'll go tell him you're here."

"I'll go myself."

The necessity of either one having to leave the room was removed by Mr. Winkler's entrance. Mrs. Winkler's slightness had led me to expect a man of lesser dimensions. Mathew Winkler, however, had the ampleness of a bulldog. Indeed, he more than casually resembled that canine. The contrast between husband and wife became greater when I noticed Mr. Winkler's look of insatiable appetites.

I immediately surmised that the poor wife wasn't up to the task of coping with such a husband, and that he found his solace wherever he could. Mathew Winkler stifled his surprise at seeing his daughter, but he was unable to completely suppress the concurrent surge of annoyance at having to force himself to hide his reaction. He shook my hand briskly, and he proceeded to lead Sharon away leaving me to Mrs. Winkler.

"Mathew hasn't seen Sharon for quite a while," Mrs. Winkler said, in what might have been an apology for her husband. But I was a stranger of unknown status, and she remembered that she need not apologize to me. "Have you known Sharon and Joseph long, Mr. Navarro?" she asked. I detected a slight inflection on the "and." I braced myself for a reprimand that failed to arrive.

"Not long," I tersely responded.

"We don't see them as often as I would wish," she continued. "The younger generation doesn't see the value of maintaining regularity in family ties. They want an easy solution to everything." She looked at me questioningly.

"I don't know about that," I said.

"Look at the rate of divorce," she said. "It's phenomenal."

"I guess it is."

"But I suppose it's better to get divorced than to have a bad marriage. Well, that's what some people say, and I agree as long as there are no children. That makes all the difference in the world. It does indeed." She stared at the wall.

"I suppose so," I said.

"Sit down Mr. Navarro," she said. "Would you like some coffee?"

"I would," I said trying to be agreeable.

She rang for the maid, who promptly appeared to take the order.

"What line of business are you in, Mr. Navarro."

"I buy and sell stocks and commodities," I said.

She seemed to mull that over for a few seconds. "You're a speculator," she said. Her voice had a sharp edge, like a blade of jungle grass that would make you bleed if you approached it at the wrong angle. I couldn't tell whether she was making a negative judgment.

"Aren't we all," I retorted.

She considered that for a moment, then she said, "I suppose so, in one way or another."

She seemed to have pulled in her fangs after that. We drank our coffee without incident until Sharon and her father returned.

"Sharon tells me you're quite a sailor," he said to me.

Sharon looked dismayed. "Daddy, don't!"

"My daughter is worried about you, Mr. Navarro. Do you need to be worried about?"

"No sir, I don't think so."

"Well good," he said. "A man who needs to be worried about is not much of a man. Isn't that so Mr. Navarro?"

"Maybe," I said.

He responded with an ambiguous grunt. I couldn't tell whether he was assenting to the validity of my maybe or being derisive. He beckoned me to follow him.

We left the women and walked down to the boathouse. I supposed he considered the outdoors a man's domain, though I surmised that he didn't allow his wife any ground at all. We walked up the steps to the second story deck overlooking the water. The scenery reminded me of paintings I had often seen in street art shows. Perhaps Mr. Winkler had hired one of those artists to come paint the background on his property, and I was now looking at the masterpiece. Perhaps if we got into one of his boats and went out on the lake, we would eventually run into the canvas. If we slashed through it, I would see the reality behind it. We sat down on a couple deck chairs on the veranda.

"I take it that you're a man of means, Mr. Navarro."

I slightly nodded.

"Well that's one good thing about this situation," he said.

"You know it would have been intolerable if you were a pauper. Still you can't expect me to be happy with your running around with my daughter." Mr. Winkler loved to be in the right, and he was afflicted with the compulsion to make others agree with his assessment of the world. "I suppose you're married too?"

"No sir, I'm divorced."

"Well, all the better. There's no reason for you to keep from marrying Sharon, is there?"

"There is one," I reminded him.

"A mere technicality," he said with a wave of his hand. "Getting a divorce these days is no problem at all, as you must know."

"It's my impression that Sharon doesn't want a divorce." I was sure that he knew that already. He was playing a game with me, but to what end, I couldn't tell.

"You should take care of that, shouldn't you? If she loves you as she says, and you love her, which I presume you do, or at least you think you do, or you wouldn't be here, you shouldn't have any problem moving her in the right direction. You must recognize your responsibility."

"Your idea of responsibility may be a bit different from mine," I said to him.

A primitive look descended on his face, animal like, but different from the one he had before, less canine. He seemed a slimy creepy thing, more like a rodent. The change made him more loathsome and contemptible.

"We're not playing games here. How do you suppose I feel seeing my daughter running around like a whore? And the two of you have the gall to come here and rub it in my face. This is beyond comprehension. Exactly what did you think you were doing when you came here?" Trying to contain his anger, his eyes became moist and the lines around his mouth tightened.

He was absolutely right. Sharon and I had no business being there together. I was in the wrong, and I knew it. That put me at a disadvantage. Ordinarily, this was the kind of situation that I handled by taking the offensive, but I was checked. If I told the truth—that I didn't even know that I was coming to the place, that it had all been Sharon's doing—I would come out looking like a fool if not a coward.

"Yes, you're right," I said.

I got up and left the boathouse. I walked up the gravel path back to the main house, but I didn't go in. I went to the car and honked the horn until Sharon came out.

"I'm leaving," I said. "You can come or not."

"Let me say goodbye to Mother," she said.

I got in the car and revved up the engine. Sharon was out in a flash. Mr. Winkler was just coming into view as she opened the car door. She waved to him, but he pretended not so see her. When she was in the car, I noticed that tears had smudged her makeup. On the road, I drove like a madman.

"Slow down," she said. She was still crying.

I slowed down. "What the hell did you expect?"

"I'm sorry," she said. "I wasn't thinking."

That made me all the angrier, because I didn't understand how she could act without thinking, especially in this case.

"Don't be angry at me," she begged. "I can't stand to have you angry at me also."

I kept silent. My anger, caught in my throat, wouldn't let any words out.

"I had this fantasy that they would be so happy to see us. I thought you would impress my father."

"Sharon, how could you think that?"

"I don't know," she said.

I figured that was true. My anger had subsided by the time we got to Gloucester. We had reservations at an inn by the sea. The gray building fit into the classic image of New

England beachfront. Once inside, the low ceilings produced a feeling of comfort and safety. After we had settled in our room, we went down to the dining room and ordered the typical seafood dinners. I gorged on shrimp, but Sharon hardly touched anything on her plate. After I had my cup of coffee, I figured perhaps a walk by the beach would cheer her up.

We left the restaurant and walked down to the shore, but she remained unusually quiet. In the distance the pale colors of the New England landscape reminded me of a Cézanne painting. The planes of the buildings on the hills above the beach contrasted with the soft forms of the clouds and the ragged outcrop of stone. The rhythmic roar of the waves soothed despite the discordant cries of the gulls. Sharon seemed crushed. I wasn't used to seeing her defeated. I had grown accustomed to the prankish person who always easily bounced back.

"I'm sorry I was angry," I said.

"Are you?"

"I am."

"I'm the one who should be sorry."

"Let's both be sorry, and let it go," I said.

"Someday he'll die, and I'll be free of him."

"Be free now."

"Maybe I thought you'd kill him. Maybe that's why I took you there. But that would have been too easy. I think I'll have to do it myself." She paused, then followed with, "You're shocked."

"I'm not," I said.

"You're lying."

"I'm lying," I said.

"When I was fifteen my mother had a nervous breakdown," Sharon said. Her voice seemed very distant, as if she were talking to someone other than me. "I was very frightened. She was away for a while at a sanatorium. I felt guilty. I thought her illness was my fault. At night I used to cry myself to sleep. My father wasn't in any great shape either. He began to drink. He would get so drunk he would pass out, and I would be all alone. Sometimes he had violent fits. I was in constant fear."

A cool breeze began to blow off the ocean. A young woman ran along the water, a huge Irish setter by her side. I watched them get smaller, receding into the distance. The water like a hungry tongue eagerly lapped over the sand erasing their footprints.

"My mother was away for six months. Life was hell while she was away. When she came back, it was even worse. She still had to deal with him while she was trying to recover. That was the first time I ran away. It took them weeks to find me. You're so silent," she added in a panic.

She ran down the beach, back in the direction we had come. I followed closely behind. The path turned uphill through a clump of pines, away from the inn. She moved briskly. I stayed at a respectful distance, waiting for her to run out of steam, but I didn't want to fall too far behind. It was hard to see in the twilight. Trees surrounded us, but we hadn't moved far from the ocean. I could hear the breakers on one side. The steady rhythmic sound of the waves made me anxious... Where was she going? Her movements swift and unhesitating gave me the impression that that she was well acquainted with the path, though she had not mentioned having been there before. Perhaps I was only imagining her resolve.

The trees gave way to sky. Now I could better make out her figure in the twilight. She came to a sudden halt. I suspected that we were now considerably above the beach and that there was a sharp drop in front of her. It was too dark to have come up for the view, unless she merely wanted to look up at the moon. If she wanted to jump, I was too far off to grab her. The prudent thing to do was to talk to her calmly and not instigate any rash action. That would also keep me from seeming too much of a fool, if indeed she had only walked up there randomly.

I called out her name, but she didn't respond. My throat went dry, and I had to make an effort to keep my voice from screeching. She must have sensed my anxiety. I started whistling "When Irish Eyes are Smiling." I don't know why, neither one of us was Irish. The tune just came. Her back was still to me. I couldn't tell whether my musical virtuosity was having any effect on her. When I was close enough to put my arms around her, she turned and held on to me tightly. In a few moments she was trying to pull me down to the ground.

"Not here," I said, "the ground is rocky."

"Under the pines," she said and led the way.

Chapter 13

I HAD TO LET GO of the past. At present, I had to deal with another predicament. I had to come up with a scheme to preserve Mundo's tough guy image while getting Max off the hook. That should have been simple enough except that I had been away from the South Bronx for so long that I had forgotten the common markers. I needed a refresher course. I rummaged my brain for some practical way of solving the problem; then I remembered cousin Santiago.

I hadn't seen him for a while. I had kind of given up on him, even though some time back I had gone against my mother's advice and had hired a lawyer to defend him after one of his transgressions. That time he got a light sentence, but the next time he got caught I realized my mother was right. Santiago was a black sheep. Still, he was one of the family. Aunt Felicia, his mother, was also an odd bird, blind to the adversities of life. Through many of the ups and downs, she kept a smile on her face. For her, happiness was divorced from the physical world. The more absurdly she behaved, the happier she looked, regardless of the consequences. That attitude drove my mother batty, but there was nothing she could do about it, and eventually she accepted her sister's condition as permanent.

On the phone, Santiago sounded thrilled to hear my voice, and when I explained to him that I needed his help he became enthusiastic. Of course he would help me, he assured me. Being of any use to others in the family had become for him a means of obtaining grace, a development I had failed to foresee. Not that he reformed his ways. He was still in constant trouble. Indulging in shady business had become for him a habit.

I went up to his apartment on Faile Street, and I was somewhat taken aback when I walked into the place. It looked like a flophouse. He was obviously experiencing a downturn in the business cycle. I suppose that's the potential danger in any endeavor. In his early twenties, he still looked like a teenager with alert eyes, slim nose and olive complexion.

"So what's up?" he asked.

I sat down at the kitchen table, and I explained the predicament of trying to get Maximo off the hook with Mundo Gonzales.

"Wow, that's something," he said. "Mundo Gonzales is a tough one. Best thing is to go easy. Just do what he says."

"I want to help Max," I said.

"Sure you do," Santiago said, "sure you do."

I expected him to follow that up with some information, like the usual way of extricating oneself from such a predicament, but maybe there wasn't any. "There has to be a way out other than biting the bullet," I said. Santiago just stared at me silently, and I hoped that his brain was working on a way out.

"I don't think we have to worry about bullets yet," he said.

So maybe he had never heard the expression and the meaning escaped him. I was willing to just focus on the word *yet*.

"No, it's not that serious," I said, more to myself than to Santiago.

"I suppose he can get out of town for a while," Santiago said.

"That's a little drastic, don't you think? How long would he have to be away?"

"Till Mundo is put away, either at Sing Sing or six feet under.

"You still have a sense of humor."

"What do you mean?"

Well, maybe he was serious after all. I was getting to the point where I couldn't tell. "Never mind," I said, "I guess there's no way out of this."

"You're not the one who owes, so don't worry?"

"Well, suppose I were the one in trouble, what then?"

"But you're not the one, right?"

"Right, but what if?"

"Well, then we'd have to consult the guys down at the Cambray Club."

"So let's go consult them."

"Max isn't a member."

"Well, neither am I."

"Yeah, but you're my cousin, so that covers you. After all, we have the same grandparents."

Cambray was the neighborhood in Bayamon where our grandparents had ended up after moving from the mountains to the city. These guys had never set foot in Cambray, probably didn't even know what part of the city it occupied or whether it still existed at all, so why they named the club after such a place still puzzles me.

"So let's go," I said.

"Nobody's there right now," Santiago reminded me.

Of course, that made sense. A meeting would have to be called if the club was to be consulted. There wasn't enough time for that.

"Yeah, you're right," I said. "I have to figure something out on my own."

"You worry too much," Santiago said. "This guy was a boxer, right, so a few blows won't be anything new to him.

"Yeah, that's one way of looking at it," I said. "But he's not as young as he used to be."

"Then he should've known better."

That was the old adage. Wisdom was supposed to come with the years, but I had yet to find any evidence of that.

"Why are you so concerned about this guy, anyway? He's just the doorman at your place. What's the big deal?"

That was a good question to which I had no ready answer. I figured I'd just store it away and dig it out some other time when I had more leisure to sit around and contemplate the vagaries of life. Right then I had to deal with the more practical task of saving Max from a trashing. I appreciated Santiago's effort to look after me, but there wasn't much I could do to keep myself from being involved. The path had become unavoidable. I might have lived somewhere else, never moved to Fifth Avenue, never met Max, but who's to say that I wouldn't have gotten into a similar predicament somewhere else? Maybe my life was a sequence of events with the same results regardless of how much I tried to make it different.

"I can get the guys together by tonight," Santiago assured me.

"I need to come up with something, the sooner the better."

I didn't think they were going to come up with anything. Mundo Gonzales wasn't the kind of guy they could intimidate. Possibly someone in the group had some dope on Gonzales that might be useful. Maybe he had a rap sheet. But so what, how would that help?

When I got home, I thought of calling Romanelli. Maybe he had some connection in the Hunts Point precinct. They could harass Gonzales, but that wouldn't be of any help to Max, probably just make things worse. I called Romanelli anyway on the off chance that he might come up with some useful suggestion.

"There's nothing we can do before the crime happens," Romanelli first said. "Max can get trashed; then he can press charges, but who knows what may happen. Why don't you just stay out of it?"

"That seems to be the general opinion."

"I would go with it, if I were you."

"You know anybody up at Hunts Point that may have shit on Gonzales?"

"I'll make a call and get back to you," he said.

I spent a restless night trying to come up with some answer to the problem. I tossed for a while. Finally, I fell asleep and dreamt. Sharon appeared in the dream more beautiful than ever. My predicament amused her. I would have been uncomfortable had someone else been laughing at me, but Sharon's happy face, devoid of mockery, soothed me. "I'll tell you the answer," she said. I was sure that she had the solution to the problem, and I waited for her to tell me. Her offer to help proved that she still loved me, that she would love me forever. She was about to speak when I suddenly woke up.

At that point I had a real reason to be angry with myself. The key was somewhere inside of me, and Sharon was willing to help me from wherever she was. For some unexplainable reason I had shut her off. I tried to fall asleep again hoping that the dream would resume, and she would tell me what I needed to know. But I had no second chance that night. Did I really not want to arrive at a resolution? That would be odd indeed. I had to look deeper, easier said than done.

After breakfast, I went down to the lobby to look for Max. "I'm trying to work out a deal with Mundo," I told him. "I think he might be reasonable. He doesn't have anything personal against you, or so he says. It's just business. Not that it matters at this point, but how did you get involved with this guy, anyway? I suppose you overplayed the horses."

"The money was gambled away," he said, "but it wasn't me on horses." He launched into the story of how he had borrowed the money to help his brother convince his girlfriend to marry him. "He's crazy my brother. Why would he go to all that trouble just to get a woman? But he's my brother, so I felt compelled to help him out."

"So you borrowed the money for his wedding?"

"Not just the wedding. They wanted a new place, new furnishings and all. Of course they could get all that on credit, but they had maxed out their credit cards, and my brother wanted to take her on a honeymoon. So where do you think they ended up? Go ahead take a guess."

I figured they had gone to Niagara Falls. After all, how much imagination did they have? But I kept my mouth shut, and pretended I had no idea.

"They went to Atlantic City and lost a bundle."

"You mean your brother couldn't help gambling to impress his wife."

"Nah, I don't think it was my brother who got carried away at the roulette table."

Maybe Max had a clear sense of what had happened but maybe not. I had a hard time believing that a woman would gamble away money on her honeymoon. I figured women were more into amassing a nest egg and getting ready for the future, but I could be wrong about that too.

"I suppose you should have gone to Atlantic City with them," I jokingly said to Max.

He looked me straight in the face and with a pained expression said, "I've often thought about that."

"Cheer up Max. I have Mundo eating out of my palm. We're working on a deal to let you off the hook."

Max didn't believe me, and there was no reason why he should, but he didn't say so. You might think that I had a lot of chutzpah to lie to Max that way, but it wasn't that. I had a premonition that I was going to find the key to the problem. Everyone has a weak spot, an Achilles heel. I had to find Mundo's. I was sure that he had at least one, probably more. I just had to find the one; then everything would be all right. I wasn't going to find Mundo's weak spot sitting in my living room. I had to head back to the Bronx. I was getting ready to leave when the phone rang.

"Hey there buddy," a cheerful tone came through. It was Romanelli's voice. "Well, I have some info, but I don't know if it'll be of any use."

"Shoot," I said, which I figured was safe enough to say over the phone.

"First off, this Mundo isn't the top guy in the business up in that area, which makes more understandable his going face to face with you."

"You mean I'm not good enough for royalty."

"That's not what I said, but now that you mentioned it, I won't dispute it."

I took the comment in stride. "So who's the top guy?"

"Mundo's uncle, Sarenpillo Gonzales."

"So if I get to him, I can ask him to override Mundo's edict."

"He wouldn't want to do anything of the sort, but he does have the final word."

"It's worth a try," I said.

"No, I don't think so, but you do what you have to. Who knows what drives us, right?"

"Sometimes you're too deep for me," I said.

He laughed. "Well, keep me informed. I'll see what else I can dig up for you." After he hung up, I still heard his laughter.

With a briefcase, I went down to the bank and asked to speak to Ted Willis, the manager. He came out of his office with his hand extended, more than happy to shake mine. He was always eager to smile at the big depositors. He was ready to do whatever I asked. I could've brought in dirty money, and he would have been more than happy to launder it. He was a first class banker, and I appreciated that. Of course, I wasn't after any favors this time. All I wanted was to make a small withdrawal of twenty thousand dollars, the whole amount in one hundred dollar bills.

"No problem," he said with a wide grin. "We're here to serve."

"I really appreciate that," I replied.

Behind his gold wire spectacles, he wondered why I needed that amount in cash. A certified check was the more usual conveyance, but he restrained himself from inquiring, just as he would have done had I brought in the cash. He filled out the withdrawal slip and pushed it across the desk for me to sign; then he called in his secretary and handed it to her. She took the slip without examining it. After she turned to leave, I kept looking in her direction, her tight green dress made her figure more enticing than it would have been in no dress at all.

"Yes," Willis said, "you're a man who appreciates many things."

I just looked at him without replying. There had to be a boundary maintained in such a place of business, and he, realizing the possible misunderstanding, quickly recovered by saying, "Of course, I'm referring to your art collection, which I recall you mentioning some time back."

"Ah, yes," I said. "Art is always a comfort."

The young figure in the green dress returned with the bills in a large envelope. She had blue eyes and very sparkling teeth that she enjoyed showing off in a wide smile. I wondered whether Sharon at that age had that innocent look. The young woman handed Willis the envelope. He merely glanced at the contents, the bills bound in two sets.

"You care to count?" he asked looking straight into my eyes as if we were playing a game to see who would blink first.

"No need to count," I said as I put the money into my briefcase. "I trust the bank's efficiency." I lied about that. I was only interested in rubbing his face in my nonchalance. He desperately tried to conceal a wince, and that was good enough for me. On my way out, I smiled at the young woman and she reciprocated.

When I got up to the Hunts Point Social Club, Tuto and Pablo looked like they had not moved from the pool table since the previous day.

"You got the money?" Tuto asked.

"Maybe," I answered.

"Maybe? Maybe doesn't work around here."

"Maybe I want to speak to Don Serenpillo."

They each skipped a heartbeat on hearing the name.

"Take it easy," I said. "I won't put you down when I see him."

"You won't see him. He's retired," Tuto said.

"These days he collects Social Security," Pablo chimed in deserting his usual post in the background.

"Well, then he'll be glad to supplement his income."

"You better come in here and check what Mundo has to say," Tuto said. Having walked to Mundo's door and knocked, he opened the door slightly and stuck his head in. "Navarro wants to talk to you," I heard Tuto say.

"Oh, Mr. Navarro," Mundo's garbled voice emerged through the partially opened door. "Come in, come in, I've been waiting all morning wondering what you'd come up with to solve Max's problem."

Tuto pushed the door all the way open and stepped aside to let me in. Enough snacks covered Mundo's desk to feed a starving tribe.

"Having an early lunch today?" I asked.

"Nah, just a morning snack," he said seriously. "So tell me, what's new?"

"I thought maybe discussing the deal with your uncle might be a good idea. He might come up with an all-around acceptable compromise."

Mundo seemed cool, as he considered the suggestion. He brought an overstuffed pastrami sandwich to his mouth and took a huge bite. I figured I'd have to be patient while he chewed. I wondered how much of his income he spent on food. If he cut down a quarter and donated the money to UNICEF, starvation among the world's children might be eradicated. I refrained from telling him that. Calling up his conscience might press him up against the wall and make him unreasonable.

He swallowed his mouthful, and before taking another bite he said, "You know, Navarro, I'm getting to like you a lot. You're a smart guy, and you must be well off enough to want to spend your money on your doorman. Most people would say that's a pretty dumb idea, or maybe a little nutty, but I'm willing to look on the positive side. And maybe you're in a profitable business I might be interested in. Why don't you just forget about Max? My guys will rough him up a little and that's it. Then you and I can discuss going into some venture together. You're a Hispanic businessman and so am I, a joint effort between us is bound to be good for the community. What do you say?"

"Let's take care of Max, and then maybe we can talk business," I said though I couldn't think of any other deals the two of us could jointly undertake. Imagine him sending Tuto and Pablo to intimidate a corporate CEO with disappointing third quarter earnings. That was a whole other kettle of fish, or was it? Maybe I was the naïve one. But what the hell! Right then I had to deal with keeping Max from an unpleasant experience.

"So, you think yourself an asset to the community?" I facetiously asked.

"Of course I do," he said taking my question seriously. "A lot of people suddenly need money for unexpected expenses. Someone like you, of course, relies on the banks, but someone from this neighborhood is allowed into the bank only to make a deposit, and just imagine how seldom that is. I'm the provider of a needed service. That's what business is about. You must know that. You're a businessman yourself."

Under his definition, I suppose I wasn't much of a businessman. If I was providing a service, I couldn't exactly identify the recipient. Possibly, I was oversimplifying the matter, and the market did play a beneficial role for the everyday man walking down Southern Boulevard or Kelly Street, and if it didn't, what was that to me anyway? The market wouldn't go away just by me ignoring it. So maybe Mundo Gonzales was a credit to society while I was merely a parasite. That odd concept seemed to make sense just then, but I decided to disregard it, put it on the back burner and maybe reexamine it at a later date.

"Your uncle's input may be of some value to all concerned, an impartial opinion, one might say. So how about it?"

"And if I disagree, what then?"

"Well, then I'll have to proceed without you. Of course, I'd rather not get to that point."

"Navarro, I'm getting to like you more and more," he said and paused to take another bite of the pastrami hero that had a lot of other things between the two slabs of bread. Again I watched him chew away, and I could see that he was stalling for time to turn the tables on me. His mouth was full and he chewed for a while. A six-pack of coke rested on one corner of the desk and it still contained four cans. He reached for another can and pulled on the ring to open it. The fizzle of the escaping gas elicited a look of contentment on his cherubic face. He took a long sip to wash down his meal.

"I'll tell you what," he said. "How about if I meet you half way? Let's pretend we're in more primitive times and use an old method of administering justice, you know something like trial by fire."

He was more educated than I had figured, or maybe I was giving him too much credit. "You remember those days? You don't look that old," I said.

"The world basically doesn't change," he said. "Nowadays we have more technology to do the work, but we still have to eat and shit the same old way. Isn't that so?"

"I suppose you're right about that," I said. "So exactly what do you have in mind?"

"He's a boxer; I'll arrange a match. He goes into the ring against someone of my choice. That gives Max a fair chance to get off lightly."

"That's not fair at all," I said. "He hasn't competed professionally for a while. He doesn't stand a chance against a regular."

"Better than against Tuto and Pablo, don't you think?"

He was right about that. The concession was slight but a concession nevertheless. If I pushed to involve Mundo's uncle, I might get nothing at all.

"Okay, we're talking about someone in his weight category, right?"

"Of course, of course," Mundo assured me.

It was time to cut a deal, but I couldn't really sign on without Max's approval. "How about if we up the ante?" I said. "If Max wins, you cancel the debt completely."

"Completely? That's somewhat unfair. This whole arrangement is to cancel his delinquency fee. That's quite enough."

"Yeah, on his part, but now I'm talking about you and me. After all, I'm the one putting up the whole amount. You have the advantage in this deal. I'm taking quite a chance, right? Not only will Max get the shit beat out of him, but I stand to lose twice the amount when even the original figure is outrageous. How much did you lend him anyway, a couple of thousand? Give me a break already. You want to gamble in the stock market with me. Well, this deal would be very similar. This would be your first step into the market. Are you man enough?"

"You know, Navarro, you would make a bundle as a used car salesman. I'm getting to like you more and more, and you're making me feel guilty about taking your money, though I shouldn't, right? Twenty thousand probably doesn't mean much to you. Am I right? Of course I am. I'll meet you half way. If Max wins you give me ten and forget the penalty."

"How about if he wins, you get the JPMorgan rate?"

"You want me to be like those Wall Street scoundrels, don't you? Let me think it over. Do we have a deal?"

"Only if Max agrees," I said.

"Oh, he'll agree all right," Mundo said, and as he chuckled, his belly waggled like a mound of Jell-O.

Chapter 14

Max was still guarding the lobby when I got back downtown. I wondered how he managed the boredom of his job, just standing in long stretches of solitude, hours when not one person came in or went out of the building. I pondered how he had adjusted to the job after having had the life of an athlete. But now that he had something else to worry about, I figured standing in a deserted lobby had definite appeal. The best thing was to tell him about the deal straight out. If he didn't like the setup he could decline. I came right out with it and told him what Mundo had offered.

"That's it? Me against one of his guys?"

"Yeah," I said, "but don't underestimate who he can get to come up against you."

"In my weight category, right?"

"Sure," I said, "he agreed."

"And you took his word?"

"I'll make sure everything's by the book," I said, although I wasn't quite certain how to go about doing that. For sure, the boxing commission wasn't going to be involved. A few details about the deal hadn't come to mind until that moment, for instance, the location of the event. No doubt Mundo had some place in the Bronx in mind, but maybe a more neutral location would be preferable, if any such place existed.

"Well, I'm ready," Max said. "He never saw me fight; else he wouldn't have made the offer."

Max's confidence shook me somewhat. I had expected some reluctance and a need to persuade him. Actually, I had expected him to decline the whole deal, and I had been gearing myself to look for some other solution. I began to worry about Max's over-confidence. Preparation required a little anxiety to get it going.

"Listen Max," I said, "he wouldn't have proposed the deal unless he was very confident that his man has what it takes. So let's not assume an easy victory."

"Let me tell you," Max countered, "someone as good as me is hard to find."

Confidence has a positive side, I told myself. I figured I could depend on Agustin to knock some sense into Max and get him into shape.

"There's just one problem," Max said.

Okay, I figured I was in for it then. He had been bluffing, and he was about to let me in on the real thing.

"Carlita will hit the ceiling when she hears about this. The guys in the ring I can take care of, but Carlita is something else. She threatened to leave me if I went back to boxing."

"You're not going back as a career move," I said. "This is a one-time deal."

"One time is all she needs to go nuts," Max said.

"Well, don't tell her," I suggested.

"How will I explain any bruises to her? That ain't easy. She's not dumb, you know. She won't believe it happened accidentally in the gym, you know what I mean? She'll have a fit."

"You mean she'd prefer that they work you over rather than you get a few knocks in the ring?"

"When you put it that way, her attitude doesn't make sense, but she won't agree. Women don't think the same way men do. That's all there is to it. I don't know what to do. I'd rather get beat up than have Carlita walk out on me."

"You must be in love."

"I guess I am."

"I tell you what," I said. "I'll talk to Carlita, one more fight then you quit for good."

"She won't go along."

"She will," I said. "She'll agree to whatever is best for you."

"Maybe you're right," he said after thinking it over.

He very much doubted that I would persuade Carlita. Still, on Saturday I went up to Max's place to face her. She was very happy to see me, and she thanked me profusely for having helped Max out of his predicament. At first, I thought Max had beaten me to the punch and had explained the arrangement to her, and miraculously, she had seen the light and had agreed to go along. This misperception had a short life, and I soon realized that she hadn't the faintest idea of what was going on. Before I said anything more she picked up that my visit had a more than casual purpose.

"What now?" she asked. "You guys haven't told me everything, have you?"

"Carlita don't get over excited," Max pleaded. "It's not good for you. You know that. Just relax."

"Tell me what's going on," she demanded.

"Well, Carlita," I started out, "some problems have solutions that seem more complicated than they really are, if you know what I mean?"

"I don't know. Tell me."

"Well, we had to work out a deal with Mundo Guzman."

"I know," she said, "to pay him what we owe, right?"

"Right," I said, "but there was a penalty fee that can't be paid in cash."

"Max isn't gonna do any job for him. What if he gets caught, what then?"

"No, no, it's nothing like that," I assured her. "Everything's perfectly legal," I said stretching the truth a bit. "It's just one boxing match and that's it, one and no more."

She screamed a "no" in a pitch that practically pierced my eardrums.

"Jesus, Carlita be reasonable," Max begged. "You know I have to get out of this mess the best I can. If I don't fight, they'll have a gang after me. Does that make sense?"

She looked at Max then at me to see which one of us would tell her that we were just joking and that Max didn't have to fight anybody. "I knew you wouldn't give up boxing. You're obsessed with it. I can't take it, Max. I'm gonna go stay with mom."

"Be reasonable," Max pleaded. "I need you now more than ever."

"You should've thought of that before you went around helping your skuzzy brother," she said. She had a point there.

"Brothers are brothers," Max said. "We can't turn our backs on each other."

"Would he do the same for you?" she screamed. "You're beyond hope. You let him twist you whatever way he wants." With that she walked out, slamming the front door behind her.

"Well, that's that," I said.

"Yeah, I ain't fighting," Max said. "I'll take my chances."

"Don't be a fool. She'll be back. She just needs to blow off steam," I explained to Max as if I knew Carlita well enough to predict her behavior.

"You don't understand," Max said. "She doesn't see the world the way we do. We don't make sense to her."

About that, he was right.

Chapter 15

Max's problem was potentially minimized, and maybe I was getting a break also, but maybe not. According to the papers, the police had made an arrest in the Hobart case. They were sure they had their man, Craig Macully, a stagehand at the Village Repertory. I should have been glad, but it all seemed too simple. The pieces didn't quite fall into place for me.

Macully was the last person to be seen with Sharon. They had been riding together in the backstage elevator. His fingerprints were found on the roof near the area from where Sharon had been hurled, her hands tied with the type of rope used for stage work. He could not satisfactorily account for his whereabouts during the time of the murder. That sounded like a pretty good case, but I wanted more. The autopsy ruled out rape; yet the police ascribed sexual motives. Theoretically, she had resisted and he became enraged and killed her. That was plausible enough, and yet I couldn't rid myself of the notion that Sharon was too sophisticated to have made enough wrong moves in that scenario to end up dead.

I needed more information about this Macully before I could lay my doubts to rest. I decided to call Harry Greenberg, assistant to the artistic director at the theater. He was also a second cousin to my ex-wife. In general, her relatives were capital people. Harry was one of the best. He and I didn't see eye to eye about everything in theater, but then we all have our private lunacies. I called him at his office, but he wasn't in. He called back in the evening.

"How are you Marco? We haven't seen you in ages. I was glad to hear from you. Sorry I didn't get a chance to call you back till now. I'm drowning in work. If it's not budget problems, it's temperamental actors, and just when you think you're going to have a rest something else turns up. And now this unfortunate incident has everyone on edge."

"Unfortunate incident" hardly seemed an appropriate term for a murder. I resented this sanitizing of reality. Of course, it would seem merely an incident to most people, but I expected more from Harry.

"That's what I want to talk to you about," I said.

There was an awkward silence at the other end.

"Harry, are you there?"

"I'm here," he said. "What's your interest in this?" His voice had taken on an executive tone.

"I knew Sharon Hobart," I said. "I'm about to write an article, maybe a book, about her. I want to understand her death before I can put her life into perspective. So I was wondering whether it would be all right for me to take a look around the place, try to follow her path that last day. Ask a few questions. Nothing obtrusive, you understand. I'll be as discreet as possible."

"I'd like to oblige you, Marc, but this thing has everybody upset already. I just want to let everything settle down."

"I promise you, Harry, discretion is my byword."

After another pause he said, "Okay, when are you coming?"

"Tomorrow," I answered.

The next day I went straight to the theater. It wasn't much of a walk from my place, and I figured I needed the morning exercise. I avoided Eighth Street, no longer what it used to be. It had become replete with shops that catered to a taste in the bizarre. I turned the corner on Lafayette and walked briskly to the front entrance and up the short steps to the fancy doors. I entered the grandiose lobby, marble floors and high ceilings. I looked around for an elevator or a stairway up to get to the offices on the third floor. As I wondered which way to turn, a security guard approached me. "May I help you?" he asked in a tone that belied the meaning of the words. It would take more than that to intimidate me.

"I'm trying to figure out how to get to Harry Greenberg's office," I said.

"Are you expected?"

"I spoke to Harry last night. He's getting older, but I don't think his memory has deteriorated that much."

He retrieved his cell phone and called upstairs. After my claim was verified, he told me to go outside again, proceed around the corner. The employee entrance would lead me to an elevator that would take me up to Harry's office. Of course, Harry could have told me all of that when I spoke to him the night before, but he didn't. I went out to the street again and walked around the corner. I found the staff entrance, went in, and I ran into another security guard before I got to the elevator. He was a lot friendlier than the first guy, and he called Harry's office to let them know I was on my way up.

The green carpeting upstairs was easier on my feet than the marble in the lobby had been. Harry sat behind a mahogany desk. In his late fifties, white streaked his hair, both on his head and face. He stepped from behind the desk to greet me with a vigorous handshake, like a politician making his rounds. I explained again that I was doing a piece on Sharon Hobart, possibly for the Sunday Times but that there were some magazines interested also. I had in fact called several places with the proposal, just in case Harry decided to check up.

He led me out to the hallway where, Linda, his young

secretary, sat at her desk. She wore a great deal of eye shadow and very red lipstick. She was very taken with being Harry Greenberg's secretary. I presumed she was competent. He instructed her to show me around and to give me all the information I needed.

"I'll take you down to the theater," she said. "Then we'll go backstage."

I followed her.

"This murder was just awful," she said. "You wouldn't expect such things to happen in a place like this. It just makes you fear the whole world. I mean, you would expect a theater to be safe, wouldn't you?"

"I know what you mean."

"I suppose you do," she said giving me a suggestive glance, the meaning of which escaped me. We went down to the pit. It was deserted.

"Are these chairs and music stands out here all the time?"

"No, of course not, but there's a rehearsal this afternoon, so they're out." My ignorance of everyday theater procedure appalled her.

"I see," I said.

"Sharon went backstage during the second act, because she wasn't on."

I followed Linda to an elevator in the rear.

"She took the elevator down," Linda said.

"How do you know she took the elevator down?"

"She was seen. There were plenty of people back here. That's how the police got the composite of the killer."

"And who is the killer?"

"Craig Macully, of course. Don't you read the paper?"

"Some people don't think he did it. I was just wondering whether you're one of them."

"Well, of course his friends don't think he did it, but they're just trying to cover up for him. He did it all right.

He's a druggie, isn't he? They're capable of anything." She gave me a knowing look. "He took her up there to have his way with her. I shudder when I think about it."

There was a pretty face under the makeup. I wanted to give her some advice, but I restrained myself. "She wasn't raped," I said.

"Yeah, he probably couldn't do it once he got up there. That's why he killed her. He got into a rage, because he couldn't do it."

"I see," I said. "Did you ever meet Craig Macully?"

"Nah, I don't hang out with the stagehands. I work in the office," she said emphatically.

"No, I guess you wouldn't get much of a chance to go backstage," I said.

"Oh, I get back there plenty," she said. "I just don't hang out there. I mean, I don't socialize with the stagehands. After all, they're nothing but glorified furniture movers, aren't they?"

"Well, that's one way of looking at them."

"Of course, there's one of them that's kind of good looking and sweet. He tries to talk to me sometimes. I just know he wants to ask me out, but he's too shy. I don't encourage him though. I mean, a stagehand is just not the sort for me."

"You think I can get to speak to some of those stagehands, someone who knows Craig Macully?"

"They're not in yet," she said, "but if you wait around, you'll see them. They'll have to start setting up for tonight's performance pretty soon. I'm sure they'll be glad to talk their heads off to you. I wouldn't believe anything they say, though. They'll just try to defend the guy. They don't want to get a bad reputation, you know. That's why they don't want to believe Craig did it."

We got into the elevator and rode down to the lower level.

"What's down here?" I asked.

"Just storage."

"Why would Sharon come down to the storage area?"

"She wasn't," Linda replied pertly. She seemed to have thought enough about the incident to be sure of all her answers. "She was going down to the dressing room. I think one of her fellow actors was more than a friend."

"And Miss Hobart's assignations were common knowledge around here?"

"She was pretty hot stuff, if you believe all the talk."

"So you think Craig got a hold of her when she came down here?"

"Of course."

"Then he took her to the roof? If he wanted to rape her, why didn't he do it down here? It seems an ideal place. The roof is a long way from here. Why would he take the chance of being discovered on his way up?"

"During a performance there's more traffic down here than there is on the stairs," she said. She was getting impatient with my ignorance. "No one ever takes the stairs in this building. I mean, you'd be crazy to use the stairs. Hey, you know something?"

"What?"

"For a friend of Ms. Hobart's you sure find a lot of excuses for her murderer. You're making him seem innocent."

"Not me," I said. "I want the guilty to suffer. I'm going to go up the stairs to the roof. You don't have to come if you don't want to climb all those steps."

"I don't mind," she said. "Actually, I've never been on the roof. It'll be kind of interesting."

When we got to the top of the stairs, we unbolted the door to the roof and walked out unto the flat expanse. Linda led the way. She seemed to know exactly where she was going.

"Ah, over there," she said pointing to a metal hatch cover. "That must have been where he threw her down."

I lifted the hatch cover and looked down. I felt woozy. There was a weakness in my knees. I pulled away from the opening.

"Mr. Navarro," Linda shouted. "Are you all right?"

I heard her voice clearly, but it seemed to be coming from far away. Sharon was still alive, I kept thinking, she was still alive when he threw her down.

"Mr. Navarro, are you all right?"

No, I wasn't all right. I would never be all right again. My stomach became the focal point as it tried to turn inside out and regurgitate my breakfast. The girl held me by one arm and walked me away from the opening.

"Come on let's get away from here. You need a drink to calm you down."

"I need more than one," I said.

We walked down one flight; then we found an elevator that took us down to the lobby.

"Let's go for the drink," I said.

We went out of the building and walked down to the corner. There was a lot of traffic on Lafayette at that time of day. We crossed the street to O'Neil's. I ordered a brandy. She had Perrier.

"I have to go back to work," she explained, "and alcohol makes me sleepy."

I nodded my head. The brandy went nicely, made me feel warm inside.

"The color is coming back to your face," she said.

"Yea, I feel better."

"You're not as tough as you pretend, are you?"

"I guess not."

"Did you know Sharon well?"

"I knew her."

"I guess you don't want to talk about it. Are you really writing an article or are you trying to do something else?"

"I'm writing an article," I said.

She looked unconvinced but willing to humor me, the maternal side of her coming out. Now that she had seen how tough I wasn't, she had decided that I needed looking after. I felt flattered, but it was her fantasy, not mine.

"You know I can help you," she said.

"You can help me do what?"

"Whatever it is that you're doing."

"Writing an article," I reiterated.

"Yeah, I can help you. I can do research or whatever. I can snoop around here and find things out, whatever you want to know."

She was brighter than I had surmised. "Hey, all I'm doing is trying to write an article, and I do my own research."

"Have it your own way," she said.

"I always do."

She looked peeved. Her movements became more angular, and her words well-padded with silences. I hadn't meant to offend her. She was a nice kid.

"Hey, don't go sour on me," I said.

"Who's sour? You're the one who wants to be tough. Listen, it's all the same to me. I'm just trying to be helpful."

"I know," I said, "and I appreciate it, but right now I don't even know what I'm looking for. I don't want to get you involved in anything that has to do with a murder. It wouldn't be fair, would it?"

"What does it matter? The killer is in jail."

"That's right. Still, I wouldn't feel comfortable."

"Because you don't think Macully is the killer."

"I didn't say that."

"Well, I'm still willing to help. She took a pad and a pencil out of her purse, and she scribbled something. She tore the paper out of the pad and handed it to me. "Here's my number," she said. "Just call me when you need me."

For a minute, I feared she would ask me for my number, but she didn't. I guessed she had already figured there were easier ways to get it. I sat back and indulgently smiled at her.

O'Neil's wasn't crowded, but there were enough people to make me wonder why they weren't somewhere else. At any hour of the day, one could look in any number of bars and coffee shops to find an incredible number of people just hanging out, so many people not visibly employed, moreover hanging out in places where they had to spend money. Doubtlessly, not all these people were wealthy, but neither were they poor. I was one of them at the moment. Sometimes I became a little disgusted with myself. Not that there was anything intrinsically wrong with me in particular, but there seemed to be something wrong with whiling away time in frivolous pursuits without having to work. For sure my freedom was being bought at somebody else's expense. Normally, I tried not to think about that, but sitting in a bar made that difficult.

Of course, I was exaggerating somewhat. I looked at Linda sitting across the table from me. She was in a bar but working. Spending the afternoon with me was part of her job. That included drinking Perrier at O'Neil's. What was so terrible about that? Nothing, maybe—or only a little.

"You look depressed," she said. "Maybe you should just forget this whole thing with Sharon. She's dead. There's nothing you can do about it."

"Oh, I wasn't thinking about Sharon," I said, but I wasn't quite sure that was true. "I was just looking across the street. There's something depressing about that place."

"The theater, you mean?"

"Yeah."

"The Repertory is not to blame for what happened to Sharon."

"Isn't it?"

"Of course not," she said.

We went back to the theater, though I didn't really need to talk to the stagehands. I had gotten enough information from Linda. She was right about one thing: those guys weren't going to talk straight, or so I thought. But I had nothing to lose but time, and I wasn't too concerned about that. At a quick or a slow pace, I was going to get to the bottom of this.

Linda introduced me to the crew chief. He pointed out some of Craig's friends. One of them didn't want to talk, but he hung around listening to what others said. There was a talkative one, a friendly sort with an open face. He was confident that he could handle whatever he took on.

"So what are you writing?" he asked.

"An article about Sharon Hobart."

"You write for one of those scandalous sheets, like the *Enquirer*? You're looking for dirt or you're looking for facts?"

"I'm looking for truth."

"No kidding?"

"That's right."

"I'll tell you the truth. This thing is a frame-up."

"You can't believe a friend of yours is a killer?"

"A killer? Craig Macully couldn't kill a fly. He hasn't got the stomach."

"You mean he's not man enough."

"I didn't say that."

"But that's what you meant."

"Maybe."

"That's just the kind of guy who would go after a woman.

He might not be able to handle a man, but he could kill a woman."

"Macully couldn't have killed anybody, even if he wanted to, not on that day anyway. He wouldn't have had the strength."

"No?"

"No, he was too drunk. He was down there in the basement sleeping it off. Besides, he has an injured arm. He wouldn't have been able to kill her the way they said he did. She wasn't a frail little woman. It must've taken some doing to kill her."

"With all this evidence in his favor, why do you suppose the police arrested him?"

"I'm telling you it's a frame-up. It doesn't look so good if they don't arrest somebody."

"Okay, thanks a lot," I said.

I wanted to say goodbye to Harry, so I accompanied Linda back to the office.

"See, just as I told you," she said. "They'll defend him to the end."

"Just one of them was doing the defending, and he seemed to have logic on his side."

"Not enough," she said. "I'm convinced Macully is guilty."

"Well, maybe you're right."

"I know I am."

Harry wasn't in his office when we got back, and I didn't feel like hanging around. I took my leave of Linda.

"Don't forget to call me," she said.

I nodded ambiguously and waved.

Chapter 16

SOME NIGHTS I COULDN'T sleep. I stayed up thinking about Sharon, about the good time we had. We hadn't had much of it, but we had made the best of it, as if we knew all along that it wasn't going to last. If she had lived, maybe we would have grown tired of each other eventually. The best relationships have a way of going sour.

I'm unlucky with women. My marriage to Gail ended in nothing, doomed from the beginning. All the signs had been there, but I didn't recognize them. We were only kids then. We were trying to do what we were supposed to. We thought we loved each other, so we got married. Sex was never great with Gail. She was so frightened. I should have known after our first attempt that it wasn't a go, but I hate to give up on anything once I've started. It seemed to me at the time that any obstacle could be overcome. I thought it would get better after we were married. That was the common wisdom or what passed for it. I thought all women were like that. What did I know? I was only a kid. There was a period when I thought things were getting better, but it didn't last long.

With Sharon sex was perfect, as if we had been made for each other, and it would never be right with anybody else. But there was a shadow over us, some secret that sometimes escaped from its prison and haunted her. She would withdraw from me suddenly. Unexplainably, she would recede into a different universe, a place inaccessible to me. I reacted puzzled and hurt. Her being married to someone else wasn't conducive to tranquility, but that wasn't what bothered her.

In July, Sam Rikenback, another member of the poker set,

had gone abroad for the summer. He had long been planning a tour of Europe, especially Italy. He had a passion for renaissance art, but he had never allowed himself to indulge it. He was too busy working all the time. He was working himself into an early grave, and his doctor told him to take a rest. So he packed up and took off for Europe with his family: his third wife and her two children. He didn't have children of his own, and that was another source of chagrin. The vacation was good for him, and it was good for me too, because for the duration he turned his place on Fire Island over to me. I didn't have a summer place. I always rented when I wanted to get away from the city, which wasn't that often. Normally, I would have told Sam to give the place to someone who would appreciate not having to pay for it, some poor artist who would be eternally grateful. But the relationship with Sharon blossoming, a place to escape from the city whenever we needed to was convenient. Sam's trip saved us the trouble of having to look, and besides, that late in the season it would have been hard to find a convenient getaway.

The house was too big for two. It was too big for four. Sam's wife liked to entertain, so they had a large house, and she constantly filled it with people. Sam was hardly ever there; he stayed in the city and worked. It was a sumptuous enough house in the modern style of interlocking planes and a great deal of glass. It was on the bay side of the island in a row of equally impressive houses. That strip was labeled "The Gold Coast."

It was a short walk to the ocean side of the island. I'm not much of a beach person, but Sharon loved it. I went there for her sake. Actually, she would fend for herself most the day, while I tried to work. I was on the phone a great deal to my broker in New York and to the commodities man in Chicago. I was also trying to finish a couple of stories. But every once in a while, I would lose my urge to stay busy, and I would saunter down to the beach to look for Sharon.

Fire Island was not my favorite place. The landscape didn't agree with me. It was too flat, too barren. I tried to appreciate what other people saw in it: the sea, the dunes, in some areas the high grass, but that wasn't my kind of scenery. Anyway, I don't think most people go to Fire Island for the landscape. Sharon went for the sea, and I went for her.

The houses on the island were, for the most part, unimpressive, the ones on the "gold coast" the exceptions. After a while, every town seemed to me a collection of shacks. I tried to concentrate on the quaintness of it all, and when that failed, I gazed at the ocean.

I got into my swimming trunks and walked down to the beach. The boardwalk felt pleasantly warm under my bare feet. I carried my flip-flops in one hand reserving them for the sand that I knew would be hot. I heard the sound of the surf just over the next dune, seagulls squawked overhead. When I got within sight of the water, I scanned the beach for signs of Sharon. She was nowhere to be seen. I walked down to the water and strained my sight trying to make out the swimming figures in the distance. Two specks hovered way out beyond the power of human sight to distinguish, but I doubted that one of them might be her. She wouldn't go out that far with a stranger, not after Charles' accident and the assault on me.

I walked down the beach for a bit. Mostly women populated the beach during the week. The men came on the weekend. There wasn't much to look at though. I walked for about twenty minutes, my feet in the surf. Every once in a while I glanced out at the distant figures in the water. By the time I turned around to walk back, they seemed to be getting closer. Finally, I recognized Sharon. Getting back to where I had started my walk, I waited for her to come out. When she saw me, she flashed a big smile. I didn't return it. I was too preoccupied with the hulking young man coming out behind her. He seemed the sort husbands ought to worry about, but I wasn't the husband after all. There was something else about him that bothered me. I didn't know what, and that made me all the more morose.

"This is Steve Collins," she said to me, and to reassure me, she leaned her body against mine.

I stretched my hand out to Steve. He had a firm grip. After some small talk about swimming, he seemed a monosyllabic person, he went his way, and Sharon and I went ours. Sharon ran her hand up and down my back as we walked to our beach blanket.

"You went pretty far out," I said, "with a stranger."

"You're jealous," she said with mirth in her eyes.

"I'm not," I said, but I was. "You have to be more careful. What if somebody is out to get you?"

"Why would somebody be out to get me?"

"You know that better than I. Why did somebody get Charles?"

"I thought we weren't going to talk about that anymore."

"We weren't, but you're forcing me."

She was pensive for a while. I waited for her to break down and tell me everything. She was on the verge, but she changed her mind suddenly, as if she had remembered some reason why she had to remain secretive. She threw her arms up around me and pulled me down. She held me until the tension left.

"This is a family beach," I said.

"I don't care."

"Let's go home."

"It's too far," she said. "There's some high grass just on the other side of the dune."

"You're crazy," I said.

She pushed me off the blanket, got up, and gathering the blanket, headed for the tall grass. She ran up the dune. I got up and followed her. When I caught up to her, she had found a clearing. She spread the blanket and sat down. I looked around nervously.

"No one can see us," she said.

"Come sit next to me," she implored. "There's no harm in that" she said, mocking my prudishness.

"Isn't there?" I said complying. I don't know why I let her get away with manipulating me that way. No other woman could have done that to me. Well, not many others. She lay back on the blanket and ignored me for a while. The fabric of her bikini strained against her flesh as she provocatively moved her legs. I felt pretty stupid, torn between my desire and my fear of being embarrassed.

A couple of days later, Sharon came in with a grin on her face. "I met an acquaintance of yours on the beach," she said. Her tone of voice told me she was up to no-good.

"Yeah, who? Hank Wilson, the child robber baron?" Hank had a house about a mile down the beach. I had met him at the sailing school and got to like him. We both liked sailboats. He was a young man but ruthless as hell. He had inherited a hardware store and had parlayed that into a multi-million dollar business. That's what I call aggressive. In general, I don't get on with guys like that, but Hank had a disarming charm, although I was perfectly aware that he was the kind of guy who would make a play for Sharon just for the hell of it—to see if he could beat me at something.

"Who's Hank Wilson?" she asked.

"Nobody in particular," I said. "Just a guy I know."

"No, it's not him," she said. "It's a surprise. I invited the person over this afternoon. I hope you don't mind."

"I love surprises," I said making up my mind to be pleasant no matter who it was.

Around three o'clock I heard someone talking to Sharon out back. I put my writing aside and prepared to meet my surprise. Sharon was already serving ice tea when I went out to the deck to meet the person.

"Hello Marc. Don't look so stunned," she said. It was Gail, my ex-wife.

"Gail!" I exclaimed. "What a pleasant surprise!" It was easy enough to pretend.

I tried to read some purpose in Sharon's face, but she was playing inscrutably straight. Perhaps she wanted to see how Gail and I interacted in order to figure out why I had ever married her. I often wondered about that myself, my marriage one of those inexplicable mistakes forever a mystery to the participants. Gail was not a bad looking woman, although she couldn't be said to be a beauty. She possessed a certain coarse charm, the dark type, her body chunky, earthy. She reminded me of pieces of clay thrown together by a sculptor with some intention of forming a figure but forgetting and never finishing it, never quite articulating the transition between the different parts. I always had the impression, while looking at her, of subtle misalignments, slight disproportions.

"So, what have you been doing with yourself, Gail?" I asked. I didn't expect to hear anything sensible.

She began to talk about her singing career. She was taking lessons, involved with this and that chorus. Her voice burned with fervor, with dedication. Nothing could be more sublime than to dedicate one's life to performing. I had heard it all before, about writing, about photography, about dancing. At some point in her life Gail had been totally devoted to each of those arts and believed herself quite on the way to becoming one of the greats at each of them in turn. I listened indulgently. If a person was ever born without any artistic talent, that person was Gail. She persisted, however, in pursuing the futile. She was a master of self-deception.

"Singing must be really wonderful," Sharon exclaimed. "You must let us know of your next performance, so we can go hear you."

"That'll be great," Gail said. "Sure, I'll let you know. I'm working with a wonderful group."

She looked at me accusingly, as if I had failed to encourage her to indulge in her fantasies. I didn't defend myself. I refused open that can of worms again. What was the point now? And anyway that had been a minor contention between us. The real problem was of course impossible to resolve.

"Yes, that's an invaluable part of life as an artist," Sharon said. "What would one do without the support of one's friends?"

"Indeed," I chimed.

"A friend—not too long ago, when I was ready to chuck it all in—without any solicitation, just came out and said, 'if you keep making progress the way you're doing, there's no telling how far you'll get.' I mean, this was from someone who doesn't usually toss out compliments. I was walking on air for days after that."

"That's wonderful," Sharon said.

It was painful for me to hear Gail talk that way. I guess I wanted her to open her eyes and look at her life sensibly. To what end? I don't know. She seemed to manage perfectly well in her crazy way. Her fantasies always meshed with reality just enough to keep her going, if not on an even keel, at least without capsizing.

"In the meantime what do you do for a living?" I asked trying to move on to firmer ground.

"This, that, and the other," she said. "You know, whatever I can get. Right now I'm an office-temp. The pay's not bad."

I felt a little sorry for Gail. I wished that she didn't have to worry about money. We had been divorced before I had any, though I don't think that would have made any difference in the settlement. She wouldn't have taken any money from me. In that respect, she had a great deal of integrity. She wanted to make it on her own.

Our divorce had been amicable enough. It was the preceding period of confusion that played havoc with our emotions, more for Gail than for me. Believing that being a good wife and mother was a woman's major role, she tried hard. Luckily, she didn't get to be a mother while still with me.

Back then, I was working as a sales representative for a paper company. I spent my days trying to hustle paper to the printers in New York, a tough bunch. I would get home frazzled every evening. I wasn't cut out for that kind of work, but it was a job. And what the hell, a man has to do something. Gail was busy trying to become a famous photographer. She had appropriated one whole room of our three-room apartment to use as her studio. More often than not she was in there when I got home. It might be more than an hour from the time I got home until she let go of her project.

"I'm sorry Marc, honey. I was so excited about these pictures I had to print them right away. Dinner will be ready in a minute." Gail was a great fan of the simple meal, Hebrew National hotdogs, mashed potatoes and iceberg lettuce. "I really had a good day today. I think I got some good shots—I mean really good. I want you to look at them and tell me what you think."

"I think I'll be more receptive after dinner," I said. I wanted to be fair, but I had already seen enough of Gail's photos to know that it would take a gourmet meal to put me in a frame of mind to be generous about them.

"Sure, sure, after dinner you can take a closer look, but just take a peek now, while I set the table."

I took a peek. "These are really interesting," I said.

"Say more. How are they interesting?"

"They're just interesting," I said. "The patterns of light and shade are really interesting." I was too hungry to think of anything more creative to say.

"You don't like them."

"I do. I think they're fine."

"Oh, come on, you don't have to bullshit me. If you don't like them, just come out and say so."

"Gail, I'm tired and I'm hungry. I had a hard day, and I don't want to argue about this. I love your photographs."

"I don't need this condescension, you know. What the hell makes you so smug and superior?"

I didn't know the answer to that.

"That's just the way I am," I said.

"Well, fuck you."

"That's an idle threat," I snickered.

If I had slapped her, her expression would have been less pained. I saw the fury rise to her face only to fall back into itself. Slamming the door behind her, she stormed into the bedroom. I started to cook the hotdogs just to give myself something to do. I didn't really want to eat alone. I hoped that in a few minutes she would calm down sufficiently to accept my peace offering. I was sure, however, that I was in the right. In my mind, that certainly took on more and more importance as our relationship worsened.

In bed, Gail was her best when she was asleep. Other times, she just lay there as if the life force had gone out of her and was hovering somewhere else. A dead fish would have seemed more appealing.

I began to take the receptionist at the paper company out to lunch. She was only nineteen, but she had been married and divorced once already. She had long black hair that fell over her shoulders. She must have spent a fortune on eyeliner and mascara. She had a penchant for tight clothing. Adventure beckoned and I followed. A couple of times we went to a hotel during lunch hour, but that wasn't enough time. I began to see her after work. I invented reasons why I had to be out at night.

Gail became progressively morose. I felt guilty about cheating on her, although clearly she didn't enjoy sex with me. I thought it necessary to keep up the pretense of fidelity, but I couldn't see any hope for our marriage. The affair with the receptionist didn't last long. She didn't want to get that involved with a married man, she said; I should look her up when I got a divorce.

The idea of a divorce seemed scary. I didn't want to be the one to bring it up. Anyway, things began to seem better between Gail and me after my little fling. At least we weren't at each other's throats all the time. Sex still wasn't good. I thought Gail should seek some professional help, some kind of therapy, but it was hard to bring up the subject. She had joined a women's consciousness raising group, and the members had concluded that psychiatry was just another instrument used to oppress women.

At first, I was glad that Gail had found a niche. I thought that something positive might develop from her discussing her problems. But she would come home all worked up—her moods unpredictable. Sometimes she would just cry for a long time without being able to explain why she was crying. Other times, she would begin to tell me a story from her childhood to illustrate how she had been oppressed. By the end of the story, she would be ranting and raving at me, as if I had been the one who perpetrated the offense against her. Finally, she came right out and said she would be happier without having to kowtow to me. I told her I felt the same way. I packed my personal things that very night and moved out to a hotel. After I got over the initial good feeling at being free of Gail, the reality of coming home to an empty hotel room hit me pretty hard.

In the mornings I was all right, but as the day progressed I began to feel panicky. After work, I tried to stay out as long as possible. I would have a drink with my colleagues. I would have dinner out, take in a movie. I dreaded going home to that empty room. The logical thing would have been to look for some companionship, but I didn't feel quite up to it. I thought of taking up with the receptionist again, but the thought of her didn't excite me. I remembered everything we had done together that had been fun at the time, but I had the distinct impression that she wouldn't be fun anymore.

I was in pretty bad shape when I got the phone call from Frannie Thompson.

"Oh, Marc," she said, "Gail told me what happened. You must be feeling awful. I'm so sorry."

Hearing her voice was high voltage going through my body. It jolted something inside of me, and suddenly I felt a desperate desire to see her. Till then, I had kept my distance from Frannie. I didn't always feel comfortable with her. I didn't quite understand her. She was delicate and fine. I would have thought that she would have been repelled by

Gail's brashness, or at the very least, embarrassed by it. But she wasn't. She accepted Gail just the way she was, even admired her. What I saw as Gail's crudeness seemed to Frannie strength of character.

Frannie seemed not to have anybody else to spend her time with at that moment, and she expressed a great deal of sympathy. She helped me find an apartment. She was a great fan of museums, concert halls, and jazz clubs, so we often saw each other. But she wouldn't get in bed with me.

"Oh, Marc," she said. "You really don't want me," her voice like a silk scarf being passed through a napkin ring. "You're just lonely and you think you do. It's impossible, the two of us that way. It would ruin our friendship. It just would," she said, clinching her teeth and extending her head towards me, her eyes intently looking into mine trying to convey sincerity and concern.

"I think you're right," I said. "Our friendship is what's important." I was completely perplexed by my own words. I had delivered them with complete sincerity but without believing them.

She looked relieved by my display of common sense. "We can have a good time without that," she said.

Eventually, I got over the initial trauma of my divorce. Gail and I got in touch now and again. She even borrowed some money from me once, which she insisted on paying back with interest. It was just after I had begun to cash in on the market, and I really didn't care whether she paid me back or not, but she did. She drew up a payment schedule, and she strictly stuck to it. I was impressed. I had never thought of her as a disciplined person, and when I gave her the money, I did not expect to see it again.

As I looked at Gail standing next to Sharon in Sam Rikenback's house on Fire Island, it struck me that she had not changed much over the years. Perhaps she was a little more relaxed now than she had been when we were married, but she still had a flare for making perfectly nice clothes look ill fitting.

Chapter 17

O N Sunday afternoon, I drove up to the 79th Street Boat Basin. The sun shining, I was intent on having a good time, and maybe picking up a clue or two about what the connection was between Charles' death and Allied Chemicals. The company yacht was anchored about two hundred yards offshore. A motor launch ferried the guests from the pier out to the yacht. I expected to run into the same people I had seen at Frannie's party. As I waited for the launch, three more guests, two women and a man, arrived. They were birds of a different feather. This party was going to be a little more open.

The two women looked as if they had stepped out of the fashion section of The New York Times Sunday Magazine, and maybe they had. They both were thin, flat chested and had long necks. They must have been built for speed, because they sure didn't look like they could give anybody comfort. Everything about them was colorful, from the purple makeup to their baggy pantaloons. They moved in a blousy elegance, with the total effect of labored effort. The man looked like an underdeveloped photograph, or as if he had been accidentally dropped into a concoction of bleach. One longed for more contrast. He was well built, yet he exuded a delicateness characteristic of someone overly concerned with his body. The motor launch pilot checked the guests he didn't know against a list he had on a clipboard. He knew the trio—me, he had to check. Once on board, I lost track of the three for a while.

"The rich are not like you and me," Fitzgerald wrote, and

proceeded to show that they are. He was wrong; they're not. It's not money that makes the rich different. It's something else. Something they get in the cradle. It's like a diaper rash that never goes away. They want to scratch, but they can't. They spend their lives trying to distract themselves, trying to forget their congenital discomfort. If you know that about the rich, you can stay one step ahead of them. A live band on deck played in an inoffensive Musak style. Everyone stood around holding a drink and pretending that they had nothing else to think about but having a good time. I kept looking at everyone's hands, trying to see how many times they stifled the urge to scratch where it itched the most.

I didn't bother to look for Frannie. I knew she would find me sooner or later. I leaned on the stern railing for a while looking at pretty colors produced by the refraction of light on the floating oil and other filth. I missed Sharon. She would have turned this gathering into a fun event. She was onto these people. She could play their game, and beat them at it, or maybe not. Maybe she had upped the ante to more than she could handle. Maybe that's why she was dead. I had a definite hunch that Allied Chemicals had something to do with Charles' death, and if that proved true, then there was a high probability that Sharon's death was connected to them also.

I had to find somebody who was willing to talk, and that wasn't going to be easy. I needed a collaborator. Right now I had nobody. I had to keep my eyes and ears open until I got a break. That was easier said than done, and it was frustrating. Waiting often seems like doing nothing, but they also serve who stand and wait. One thing I learned from Henry Thompson was the importance of waiting for the right moment to make a move. Another was to trust intuition. It was easier to put those things into practice when buying and selling than when trying to uncover the killer of a loved one.

There I was, leaning up against the rail of the Allied Chemicals yacht, thinking that some or all of those people were in some way responsible for the death of a person who had been close to me. I began to be a little disgusted with myself, because what separated them from me was no longer so clear. There were only several types represented here: the ruthless grasping ones, the ambitious, the desperate, and a few decadent ones.

What was I doing here, really? I was looking for a clue to Sharon's murder, I said to myself, but I knew that wasn't everything. Maybe I wasn't here for Sharon really. After all, she was dead. There was nothing I could do for her now. Was there ever a time when I could have done anything for her? Perhaps not. That gnawed at me—that I was engaged in a futile endeavor with no purpose other than to soothe my sense of failure. I was here for myself trying to redeem a lost opportunity. Or maybe I didn't have so praiseworthy a motive.

Perhaps I was here just looking for a chance to snatch Frannie away from the clutching grasp of corporate power. Had I been doing it for her sake, there might have been a glimmer of salvation for me, but I couldn't even pose as her protector; or rather, I could pose, but I couldn't ignore the fact that it was my competitive pride that drove me. Mr. Thompson's words echoed in my head, "Frannie won't live without the money." I had amassed a small fortune, without thinking that I might be doing that for Frannie, but why not Frannie? Did I want to be another Gatsby looking across the bay at the light on Daisy's dock? Perhaps that was exactly what I was doing. If I didn't watch out, I could end up like Gatsby, full of holes and just as dead. I couldn't bring myself to believe that Frannie would be as callous as Daisy had been, but why not? She was going to marry Larry Copland, wasn't she?

"You seem so far away," Frannie's distinctive voice retrieved me from my reverie.

"Yes," I said, "it seems less and less strange that the body could be in one place and spirit in another."

"Well, I want your spirit to be where your body is, and I want your body to be right here," she said.

"We don't always have a choice, do we?"

"Yes we do," she said emphatically. "Sometimes it may seem as if we don't because circumstances may be difficult, but that's when we have to use our will."

"I see."

"Don't mock me," she said. "I know Sharon's death has been hard on you, but you can't let it destroy you. You have too much going for you."

"Do I look so bad that you think I'm being destroyed?"

"You've looked better. Come on, tell me how I can cheer you up," Frannie said, and anticipating a libidinous reply, she added, "within reason."

"Tell me what you know about Charles."

"I already told you everything I know. He wasn't a friend of mine."

"He worked for Allied Chemicals."

She shrugged her shoulder to say that had nothing to do with her. She squeezed my arm. "Let's dance," she said.

She pulled me to the stern deck where the band was set up, and there were a few people dancing, though most of the crowd was just standing about holding drinks. For a moment, I had the sensation of holding a piece of cotton candy, nothing but spun sugar. Then, I looked into those dark eyes, and I knew there was something more. Was she leading me on? I couldn't imagine why she would do that.

She got really close to me. "Larry is the man to talk to about Charles," she said earnestly.

She spoke the truth there, but I didn't know quite how to

approach Larry with this subject. I didn't have anything to go on. Larry didn't strike me as the sort of man who would be impressed by my intuition. What could I say to him? "I think Sharon and Charles were killed for the same reason, so tell me why anyone would have wanted to kill Charles? It has to be someone powerful enough to be able to command professional killers. You know many powerful people, point one out."

When the number was up, leading me by the hand, she said, "Come on let's go find him." We walked along the railing towards the other end of the boat. We found Larry trying to fend off the two models that had arrived on the launch with me. He was being charming to them, and they were being boringly predictable. The two pouted a little and retreated as Frannie advanced.

"Marco wants to know about Charles Osgood who used to work for you," she said. "What can you tell him?"

"Yes, Charles, very unfortunate," Larry said exchanging his party face for one of mourning. "He was killed a while back—traffic accident, very unfortunate."

"Why was he fired from Allied Chemicals?" I asked straightforwardly, thinking that was the best tack in a situation where I held no good cards.

"He wasn't fired. He resigned."

Nobody is ever fired from the high echelons of the corporate world. When your services are dispensable you simply resign.

"Well then, why did he resign?"

"He got a better offer elsewhere."

"He must have been good at what he did, which was what?"

"He was in research and development. Yes, he was a good man. It was too bad about the accident. It was such a shock to me. I never expected him to go that way. But that's the way life is, I suppose; the unexpected is always just around the corner."

Larry's gauntness made him seem older. Not that he was a young man; he had twenty years on me, if he had a day. Every time I thought of Frannie in his arms I winced.

"What's your interest in Charles? You're not an insurance man are you?" He chuckled as if that were supposed to be funny.

"I was there when he was killed," I said.

"Oh," he said after a slight pause, "that must have been a gruesome experience."

I had him then. It was just an instant, just a flicker, hardly perceptible, but he had missed a beat. He knew something about Charles' death that he wasn't telling.

"Yes," I said, "those things always are."

"They say it was a hit and run. Drunk drivers should get the book thrown at them."

With that, I couldn't disagree. "But maybe it wasn't an accident," I said. "What I want to know is, was there anybody who wanted to see Charles dead?"

"If you ask that question, you open a can of worms. Charles wasn't always the most charming person."

"You mean he had a lot of enemies."

"He was aggressive. He stepped on many people's toes. He didn't have enough grace to get away with it."

From having observed Charles that one time, I could very well believe everything Larry said about him.

"So, how many people wanted to kill him?" I asked.

"Quite a few wanted to, but none of them would have done it. Let's be realistic, we don't go about killing everyone who's unpleasant, do we?"

"No, not for unpleasantness alone, but I'm assuming that Charles was capable of going further than mere

159

unpleasantness. Let's say he could have been unprofitable to someone."

"You've lost me," he said.

"I'm kind of lost myself," I said. "That's why I need information."

"Well, I certainly don't know of anybody who would have stooped to killing him. I wouldn't have thought he was worth the effort."

"Apparently someone did."

"Assuming he was murdered. You are sure he was?"

"Not sure at all," I said.

"Why bother pursuing such a tenuous conjecture?"

"Curiosity."

"Ah," he said, as if he understood completely.

We left it at that. Frannie sequestered him to the dance floor. I decided to look around for recognizable faces.

"Aren't you Freddie Hampton—Gladys Hampton's cousin?" a silver haired person with ruby lips asked me as I returned to the stern where the main activities percolated.

"No, I'm Marco Navarro, Annie Steuben's cousin."

"Oh," she said crestfallen.

"But why should any of that come between us?" I said. "Would you care to dance?"

"Why not?" she indifferently answered.

She danced just as indifferently. I wondered what color her hair had been before being silvered.

"You're wondering about my hair," she said.

"How can you tell?" I asked feigning surprise.

"I know your type," she said with assurance. "You try to be different. That's a recent trend among young executives, but none of them quite make it, including you. There's something deep down that always comes through no matter how hard you try to cover it up."

"Well, now that you know everything about me, tell me something about yourself."

"I'm an entertainer," she said blithely.

"I would have never guessed."

"That's because besides having a great voice I can also act very well. I'm playing the part of a frivolous jet-setter."

"You had me fooled," I said. "Whom do you know at this function?"

"Everybody," she said tossing her head.

"You don't know me."

"Not personally, but I know your type."

"We went through this already."

"I know you're in middle management, and you have a brilliant future with the company, otherwise you wouldn't be here."

"So everyone here is on the way up."

"I didn't say everybody. I said you."

"I suppose that's a compliment of sorts."

"For you, I suppose it is; to somebody else, it might be an insult."

"I see."

"Do you?"

"Oh yes, I think so."

"Now there's somebody else definitely on the way up," she said directing her glance towards a woman who was sipping a drink as she looked intently into the face of an older man who was just as earnestly telling her an anecdote. The woman, hair cut short, dressed in a most businesslike way—skirt and jacket, a bright kerchief around her neck the only concession to festiveness.

"That's Agnes Stevens," my partner said.

"How well do you know her?" I asked.

"Not well at all," she replied. "I specialize in men."

"I see."

"Good," she said.

"Tell me about your performing career," I said.

"What's to tell? I sing, I dance."

"Not very well."

"Not very well, what?"

"You don't dance very well."

"You have a way of ingratiating yourself," she said, kicking my leg.

She kept silent after that, but she got closer to me and rested her head on my shoulder. When the music stopped, she was still holding on to me. Frannie suddenly appeared to pry us apart.

"Let's go up to the bridge," Frannie said.

"My name is Lynn. Don't forget me," the singer said to me, turning a shoulder up at Frannie.

"You have a way of attracting certain people," Frannie said as she led me away.

"What people are those?"

"The kind that will be of no use to you."

"What makes you think I'm looking to use anybody?"

"You're twisting my words," she said, annoyed.

I hadn't meant to push her that far. I didn't like to get women angry at me for no good reason.

"I am," I said, "and I'm sorry."

"You're not sorry. You've never been sorry for anything in your whole life. You're trying to placate me, and I don't like your condescension."

"Frannie, what are you angry about? I said I was sorry. I know you didn't mean to say that Lynn there has no class. What did you mean to say?"

She glared at me for what seemed an interminable moment. Then she looked away to conceal her smile. She played me like a yo-yo. I kept running up that string despite myself. Whenever I reached the bottom, I made a desperate effort to stay there, but there was nothing to hang on to. I needed Sharon to keep me from rolling back to Frannie, but Sharon was gone, and I had nowhere to turn. Maybe it wasn't Sharon's killer I was looking for at all. Maybe I was only looking for Sharon. Frannie took my hand and led me to the steps. We climbed up to the deserted pilot's cabin.

"You're on to something," Frannie said. "You have some suspicions. Tell me what you're after."

"I don't know anything, Frannie," I said. I really didn't know how much I could trust her, although I had the overwhelming desire to possess her. Suddenly I understood why Odysseus had tied himself to the mast.

"I know it's been hard for you—Sharon's death I mean. Let me help you."

"They have a guy in jail," I said. "He could be the killer."

"But you think there are signs pointing somewhere else."

"I think Allied Chemicals is involved in some way, and you're involved with Allied Chemicals. We shouldn't talk about this."

"I'm not involved with Allied Chemicals," she said, wriggling her nose involuntarily. "I'm involved with Larry. It's not the same thing."

"Isn't it?"

"It's not," she injected a note of impatience.

"It's not price fixing or unfair competition we're talking about. Two people have been killed."

"Yes, I know," she said, turning away from me to look into the distance.

She was wearing her hair up. I contemplated the nape of her neck. There was something luminescent about her skin—something that made me want to touch her. My hand trembled as I raised it to her shoulder, fearing that she would jump away at my touch. Perhaps I felt that she should have recoiled, but she remained perfectly still. I enveloped her

163

in my arms. She didn't resist. She seemed slight against my body. Too excited to enjoy holding her, my whole being vibrated. The first moment is always terrible. Just as my lips were about to brush against hers, she turned her head. The move, somewhat predictable, partly annoyed me, partly relieved me. It gave me time to ease into the situation.

"This is crazy," she said. She kept her arms around me.

"I know."

"Let's leave things the way they are for now, Marc. I can't handle so many things at once."

"You're right. I shouldn't even be here. I shouldn't take advantage of your friendship this way."

"You couldn't, Marc. That possibility doesn't exist for us. Anyway, if you're right about Allied Chemicals, I have to know, don't I? Even if it hurts, I have to know." She held both my hands in hers, disengaging very slowly.

"Oh, there you are," Larry said, his lank frame encompassed by the door.

Startled, I felt the blood rush to my face. There was no way I could keep myself from feeling like a child caught in the act. Frannie, on the other hand, smiled and went to him without revealing the slightest trace of discomfort.

"Larry darling," she said putting her arm through his, "Marco and I have been having the most interesting conversation about the future of Allied Chemicals. Marc, you know, is quite a financial wizard."

"So I've heard," he said. "And I believe it too. You've quite a talent."

"Thank you," I said as gratefully as I could. I wondered how long he had been observing us. I promised to talk to him at length, at some future time, about my analysis of his company's prospects, but for the time being, I excused myself and went back to try my luck with the other guests.

In a short while, I decided that the party was pretty dull

and the likelihood of getting any more information nil. I felt very uncomfortable at having been caught with Frannie. Larry Copland didn't get to where he was by staying hit, as we used to say in the P. S. 99 playground. Sooner or later he was going to hit me back, and I had to be ready for him. Thinking about it, however, took the fun out of being at this festivity. I took the launch back to shore. When I got to my car, Lynn was sitting on the hood.

"Hi," I said. "So you got bored on the boat?"

"It looks like you did too. It took you long enough," she replied.

She was bent on being sarcastic, and assumed a critical pose as a way of seeming close.

"You should've warned me," I quipped.

"You wouldn't have listened. She has you under her thumb."

"You think so?"

"I know it. You want to be saved?"

"From what?"

"From yourself mostly."

"You can try," I said. "Hop in." I unlocked the car door.

"This is yours?" she exclaimed in mock surprise.

I was mildly curious as to how she had known which car was mine, but I didn't ask. I drove down the Westside Highway, then cut over to 9th Avenue and down to the Village. The car parked, we walked around the corner to my place. She was rather coy as we waited for the elevator. At my door, I sensed something was wrong. When I pushed, it swung open. Wham! What a mess.

"Oh, my God!" Lynn exclaimed.

The place had been ransacked.

"It's the maid's day off," I said trying to stay calm. I checked the alarm. It had been turned off.

"Oh, my God, you've been robbed."

"Let's not jump to conclusions," I said. My paintings were still on the wall. Those were the most valuable things in the apartment, but it would take a sophisticated thief to realize that. I checked the place where I kept cash. It was all there. All my clothes seemed to be there albeit not where I had left them. I checked my cameras and electronic equipment. Nothing had been taken.

"Whatever they took isn't insured," I said.

"What's that?"

"I haven't the faintest idea."

"You mean somebody vandalized the place and took nothing."

"Looks that way."

"That's sick. The world is full of perverts," she said fervently.

"Well, there are other possibilities, I said. "For instance, maybe they were looking for something that wasn't here; or better yet, they took something that I didn't know was here."

"What?"

"If I knew that, I'd be a much wiser man. Would you care for a drink?"

"How can you be so calm? Aren't you angry, upset? Someone violated your space."

"I only look calm," I said. "Inside I'm a seething volcano."

"I see."

"Do you?"

"You don't care about this place. You don't care about material things. You're looking for the Holy Grail."

"Is that bad?"

"No, only archaic."

"Spiritual things exist outside of time. Archaic isn't a word that can be applied to them. Anyway, you're wrong about me. I'm very attached to my possessions."

I called the police and reported the break-in. When the neighborhood unit arrived, they were just as puzzled as I that nothing had been taken. They questioned the doorman, but Max didn't know anything about it. He hadn't seen any suspicious strangers, and if he had seen them, he certainly wouldn't have let them into the building. Nevertheless, he was extremely apologetic to me, as if he had somehow failed in his duty. The police were convinced that it was an inside job. "Somebody you know," they said. "Somebody who has a key, because it doesn't look like they broke in. An old girlfriend maybe," one of them said winking at me. Anyway, they didn't take the case very seriously.

After they left, Lynn helped me clean up. When we had nearly finished, I realized that I had taken Lynn's presence for granted. I hadn't really considered whether she was planning to stay the night or whether I wanted her to. I must have had some plan when I invited her into my car, but it had slipped my mind. She too must have had some intention, so I waited for her to make the move. I didn't presume that she wanted to stay for the night; women often didn't even if they behaved as if they did, and visa-versa.

Chapter 18

THE NIGHT OF MAX's fight, I drove up West Street to the Henry Hudson Parkway and got off at 96th Street; I turned up Riverside Drive to pick up Frannie, who wanted to attend the event. Failing to imagine that she would insist on going, I had made the mistake of mentioning it to her. I wondered whether she was trying to expand her consciousness by rubbing elbows with the culturally deprived or whether she was merely bored on Riverside.

When I got to the Thompson's, Bella greeted me in her usual charming manner. "You know Marc, you have to take care of yourself," she said as we walked to the drawing room to wait for Frannie, who was still putting on her makeup. "You don't look well at all."

Everyone in that family was concerned with my taking care of myself. "My apartment was broken into last week. I think I haven't recovered," I said.

"Oh, no! Poor baby."

I let that slide.

"Oh well, at least your insurance will cover everything. I know that's not much consolation, but it's something. And maybe the police will be able to recover some things. Art objects are not easily disposed of, and you had such beautiful things too."

"I didn't lose anything," I informed her.

"Well, that's the stoical way of looking at it," she said approvingly. She tried to endow me with traits she admired. She knew perfectly well that I wasn't the stoic type.

"They didn't take anything," I said trying to disabuse her about my heroic qualities.

"Nothing? That is strange. Well, why break in for nothing? Or maybe it was some kind of a warning. Marc," she said, getting suddenly stern, "you're not involved with shady people, are you?"

"Of course not."

"Are you sure? I know men make all kinds of acquaintances in business. My husband used to bring home the most disgusting people, but let's not talk about that. That's all passed, thank God. This break-in is very strange. It worries me. What do you suppose it means?"

"I don't know," I said.

I didn't want Bella to get involved in trying to protect me from myself, and I didn't want to give her anything else to worry about. So I didn't tell her what I was thinking. Somebody thought that I had something that I didn't know I had. I figured it must be something connected with Sharon. I had no idea what, but whatever it was, someone believed that she had passed it on to me.

I suddenly realized that this was the only lead I had—the only card. I had to play it. There was no sense trying to guess what this object of great interest was, but I had to find out who was interested. I had to make them come out into the open. I knew they would show their hand, if they became convinced that I did indeed have what they sought. I had to put the word out that I had it, but since I didn't know what it was, or who might be interested in it, I didn't know exactly how to go about leaving word. I had to include anyone who was in any way connected to Sharon.

"I think they were looking for something specific," I said, "but whatever it is, it's not something I keep in the house. I either have it on me or it's in my safe deposit box."

"Well, what is it?

"I don't know."

"Well, if you have it on you, someone could kill you to get it."

"They'll have to," I said.

"Marc, don't talk like that."

Worrying her made me feel like a heel. I promised myself that I would make it up to her when all of this was settled. I thought about my own mother, and I promised myself to go down to see her when this was over.

Right then, I had other things on my mind, but at least one mess would be cleaned up soon enough. That night, one way or another, Max's problem would be resolved.

Paul Thompson had decided he wanted to tag along with Frannie and me, and falling into my big brother role, I initially thought a trip to the Bronx would be good for him; you know, sort of expand his horizon a bit. He walked into the drawing room with Cheryl, the one I had met when I went to hear his jazz group. He had taken the liberty of inviting her also. I chalked up her presence as a positive development.

When Frannie was finally ready, we headed for Hunts Point. We drove up Riverside to Audubon Terrace and cut across Manhattan to Macomb's Dam Bridge.

"So, this is the first time going to the Bronx for all of you?" I asked.

"I've been in the Bronx before," Frannie said, somewhat peeved. Cheryl and Paul kept quiet. Probably they weren't paying any attention to me. "I am a native of this city, for your information," Frannie continued.

"Just wondering," I said. "So where in the Bronx did you hang out?"

"I've been to the zoo," she said, "and to the botanical garden."

"What about the streets? Have you ever walked on a Bronx street, or did you just drive into the zoo parking lot?"

"Just relax," she said. "When we get there, you can pretend you don't know me."

That shut me up, and we headed down 161st Street to Boston Road then over to 163rd. Before we got to Hunts Point, we stopped by Intervale Avenue to see whether Carlita wanted a ride up to see her husband fight. I doubted that she would, and I was right. Frannie's presence didn't help. Carlita wondered why any woman would want to watch a couple of guys attempt to knock each other out. I was beginning to wonder myself.

The fight was to take place at a gym transformed into an arena. When we got there, I could tell from the crowd that the house was going to sell out though it wasn't open to the general public. Pablo and Tuto kept an eye on the door and saw that no strangers got in and that each guest paid the required fee. I left my companions by ringside, and I proceeded to the locker room where Max was getting ready for his trial by fire. Agile on his feet, he bounced around the room swinging punches at the air. Maybe he would dance his way to a knockout.

"Hey Marc," he said when I walked in, "what about Carlita, is she out there?"

I had promised him that I would try to persuade her. "I stopped by your place to pick her up," I said, "but she wouldn't come. She did wish you luck." I lied about that, and he knew it, but he didn't call me on it. For him, she kept looming over the whole event, and that was a problem. There was no way to get Max to stop, but I gave it a try. "She doesn't want you to get hurt," I said. "But if you keep thinking about her, you will; so for her sake stop thinking about her."

"You're right," he said, and he kept punching at a phantom opponent.

"He's gonna do okay," Agustin said.

He too wasn't sure about that, and I could see the doubt in his face even though Max was in good shape. Agustin had kept him on a tight training schedule for three weeks, and he was as fit as he had ever been. The only problem was Carlita's disapproval constantly on his mind. "The best fighters don't get attached to women," Agustin had once said to me, and I didn't believe him then, but now I could see what he meant.

Tuto came by to say that the crowd was ready to see some action. All the guests had arrived, and the door had been locked.

"Okay, we're ready," Agustin said holding Max's red, white, and blue robe so that Max could fit himself in. The robe matched his trunks, Max's attempt to look patriotic.

Agustin had brought a bunch of guys with him to prevent isolation in enemy territory, but really there was no need. The crowd was there to see a fight, and just as many would cheer for Max as for his rival. Max was after all a Bronx boy. The opponent had already climbed into the ring and was prancing in his corner. The guy looked more like an ox than anything else. I could see him yoked to a plow. A sledgehammer would be needed to knock him out. Max would have to dance around to stay alive. I began to regret having arranged the event, but I reminded myself that at least this way he had a chance to defend himself.

When I went to the locker room, I had left my traveling companions to fend for themselves. Of course Frannie had proceeded to do her usual. When I returned, she was sitting next to Mundo, and surrounded by a bunch of guys lapping up her charm adding another quirk to the already tense situation. "She knows her way to the top," I grumbled to myself. She had saved a seat for me next to her, for which I was grateful, and of course, all I needed was one chair, as opposed to Mundo who seemed to spread over three. Paul and Cheryl seemed to be interested only in each other.

"Ah, you're a lucky guy," Mundo said when I sat down. Frannie occupied the seat between us, and he had to lean forward to look at me.

"Well, we'll see when the bell rings," I said, and I really meant it. I looked up to see the goon at the opposite corner from Max, who continued jumping up and down as if he had not yet taken a good look at his opponent.

"About that, you're right," Mundo said, chuckling and sitting back to gaze at his fighter.

The ref walked out to the center of the ring, and each trainer patted his guy on the back and sent him out like a rooster, except that roosters don't need to pretend sportsmanship. I found out later that Trenchero, Mundo's guy, had a reputation for dirty fighting, but I had never heard of him, so I knew nothing about his style. I figured his weight might make him slow on his feet, to Max's advantage. Max probably thought so too, because without hesitating he went straight in, figuring he could dance his way out of anything. Trenchero wasn't going to play around. Right off he let Max have it. Max stumbled. Within the first ten seconds, he seemed about to hit the canvas.

"He's courageous, your guy," Mundo said over the noise of the crowd. "I got 'a say that for him."

"Ooh, he's a little dazed," Frannie said.

The last thing I needed was commentary from either Mundo or Frannie. Luckily, for the rest of the round Max managed to keep his distance. In the second round, Trenchero came out swinging with a left to Max's head. Max took it without flinching, and he responded with repeated rights to Trenchero's chin. Max had to work harder than he had anticipated, but he wasn't ready to leave just yet.

For a while he kept out of range of Trenchero's right. Trenchero missed with a left, but seemed to expect Max to retreat; instead, Max advanced to meet up with another left hook. I winced. The pain must have flowed from his chin all the way down to his toes. Max wasn't thinking. Everything requires thinking, even boxing. Of course, if you thought about it, why would you engage in such a ridiculous activity?

Between rounds, Agustin wiped Max's face. "He's a bum, Max. You can take him, but you got'a watch out. You can dance him to exhaustion. Take your time. You can outlast him."

"Okay," Max said.

"Stay calm," Agustin said. "You have to keep your cool. Don't lose your head."

"Okay," Max repeated.

From my seat, I could see Max taking everything in, a good sign. I kept my fingers crossed and switched my gaze to the other end of the ring. Trenchero's trainer looked worried, but I couldn't figure out why. Maybe he had seen something I missed. Probably Trenchero wasn't fighting the way his people thought he should. Maybe they had expected a knockout in the first round. Max was better than they had anticipated.

In the third round, Max came out swinging with two unexpected lefts to Trenchero's head. Trenchero reeled but managed to recover before Max had a chance to strike again. Trenchero responded with a low blow that landed below Max's waist. The referee didn't say anything. Maybe he missed it, or maybe he'd been bought. Agustin had negotiated to get an impartial referee, but who knows what might have happened after that. However, Max seemed to handle the blow okay, and he responded more energetically than anyone expected, especially Trenchero, who caught by surprise was driven up against the ropes and suddenly seemed exhausted.

Max moved in close, and Trenchero grabbed him as if they were wrestling instead of boxing. The crowd began to boo. Everyone wanted to see a real contest and not just a set up. Mundo passed the word up to his fighter to play it straight, something he wasn't used to. Trenchero became confused. Was he supposed to throw the fight, or what?

"Wow, Max is coming back, he's coming back," Frannie said.

I smiled thinking she was right, but I didn't want to jump to a premature conclusion. Mundo's man could come out with a whopper and unexpectedly lay Max out. Max sprung a short left to the head. Trenchero countered with a backhand. This time the referee admonished him, to the approval of the crowd.

"That's right, that's right," Agustin shouted. "Keep it clean."

Still, Trenchero had a good right and kept trying to connect to Max's face. Max avoided the blow and received only slight taps on the chin. Again Trenchero backhanded, upsetting Mundo who began to curse him out. Who was he rooting for? The crowd seemed to be on Max's side, and it was hard to go against the crowd. Trenchero charged only to be stopped by Max's jab. At close quarters Trenchero landed a couple of uppercuts, but Max just kept punching, delivered a right to his opponents jaw and made him buckle.

"Kill the bastard," Agustin shouted.

Trenchero made a sudden recovery. He rushed in swinging from both sides and landing lefts and rights. Max retaliated by pushing him up against the ropes, but Trenchero responded with a right to the jaw that knocked Max's head back. For several seconds Max's senses vanished, but they returned, and he proceeded to land a right on Trenchero's jaw. Breathing hard, Trenchero delivered two seemingly useless quick ones to the head. Everyone, especially Max, could see Trenchero's frustration. He had expected to make quick work of Max, but that was out of the question. He had to count on luck to get a knockout, but it wasn't his lucky day. To the side of Trenchero's head, Max landed a right. Trenchero's knees buckled. He reeled. He stayed down for an eight count. He got up seeming to forget where he was.

"Fight, you bastard, fight!" Mundo shouted at him.

I don't think Trenchero heard, but he automatically put up his arms instinctively knowing that he had to defend himself. Max was on a roll. He jabbed a couple of times and retreated, bouncing around as if the main thing was showing off his footwork.

"Jesus Christ, don't fool around," Agustin shouted. "Just finish him off."

This time Max went in alternating right and left forcing Trenchero, his arms up to cover his face, against the ropes. Max went for the stomach. There was nothing his opponent could do. He would have been down again, but the bell rang.

"Wow, this is something," Frannie said.

I stared into her face. Did I know her? I hadn't expected her to be so enthralled by violence. That goes to show how much I know about women. Well, I consoled myself, at least I helped Max save himself from Mundo, who also surprised me by quickly recovering from an apoplexy that invaded him the minute his man began to wane. I had the urge to gloat, but I restrained myself. The fight wasn't quite over yet. We had to get out of this gym, then out of the Bronx.

The bell rang again, and Max went in for the kill. Trenchero looked like his attendants had painted a smile on his face. If it was meant to fool Max, it failed. Max took it as a challenge and proceeded to pummel it off Trenchero's face. For a second Max retreated to evaluate his own work. Proud of himself, he moved in for the last punch. It landed right between Trenchero's eyes knocking him out for the count. Trenchero was still unconscious when the referee raised Max's arm to declare him the victor.

"He won, he won," Frannie shouted swinging her arms around my neck. I couldn't resist throwing mine around her and squeezing her as hard as I could, but all along I knew I was yet a long way from a knockout.

While I was still holding Frannie, I heard Paul say, "What happened? Did I miss the finish?"

You can't win them all, I suppose.

Chapter 19

THE DAY AFTER the fight, I felt relieved to have dealt with one problem, but the other persisted. The prey kept eluding me, and I didn't quite know what to do next. I had some pieces of the puzzle, but I couldn't put them together. I needed a link that would point in the right direction. I was still sitting at my desk looking at the stock quotes when the phone rang. A familiar voice greeted me, but I didn't place it right away.

"I've been thinking about you."

"I'm flattered," I replied.

"I have something to tell you," Lynn Fromowitz said.

"I'm listening."

"I don't want to talk on the phone. Meet me under the clock at the Central Park Zoo at one."

"All right," I said.

I was there promptly. She was ten minutes late. She looked more mature than at our previous encounter—less flaky, but I wasn't about to jump to any conclusions.

"I'm glad to see you again," she said.

I didn't say anything. We walked towards the seal pond. Taking in the scene, I looked across the quadrangle. There is something romantic about the Central Park Zoo; it's quaint. One didn't go there to see the animals; they were almost incidental, merely an excuse for calling the place a zoo. It was a unique attraction: maybe the landscaping or the architecture of the buildings, or rather their placement in relation to each other, the structures unremarkable in themselves.

The usual number of people strolled about, children with

their nannies, businessmen taking a break from their office routines, teen-agers who should have been in school, and several New York characters who would have seemed out of place almost anywhere else, but at the zoo they fit right in. The obligatory balloon man, with a bunch of helium balloons rising behind him like a peacock's tail, was there too stamping the scene with authenticity.

"Well you needn't be so reassuring," she said.

"I'm sorry," I said. "I'm not all here today."

"Don't be distant because you're afraid to be close to me," she said. "That's not what I'm after."

"It's not that," I said.

"You got a problem?"

I hesitated. She seemed a little more washed-out, a little more used up. Her face had lost the first glow of youth and was beginning to show the wear of too many mornings after the night before—a face that had been scrubbed clean too often, a face accustomed to make-up and somewhat self-conscious without it, as if a naked face were somewhat obscene.

"It's nice to see you again," I said, and I meant it, though I wasn't sure why. She looked like she might be a comfortable person for me, and I didn't have to be in love with her. I was weary of women I had to love, women who glittered in my imagination and whose images refused to take no for an answer even though their bodies were out of reach.

"I have a confession to make," she said.

Her voice sounded muted, as if coming from far off. A group of girls stood in front of a cage watching two monkeys groom each other. A cockatoo screeched an unheeded warning of approaching strangers.

"I didn't happen to just meet you at the Allied Chemicals yacht—I mean, I didn't just pick you out at random."

"I'm quite sure you have an exacting criterion," I said.

"I had seen you before, the night Charles was killed. That's why I approached you."

"Oh, Charles," I said, "he grows more interesting."

"He doesn't grow more anything. He's just dead now," her voice momentarily wavered from the cold metallic tone she had assumed.

"Yes, to be sure," I said.

A long silence followed. I guess she expected me to ask the obvious question, but my thoughts were disjointed. The balloon man was behind us now. I considered that he might not be a genuine balloon man at all—that he was a balloon man impersonator, that if I turned around quickly, I would catch him in a gesture totally uncharacteristic of balloon men, and he would be unmasked as an impostor. But what of the real balloon man, where was he? If I turned around, that might remain a mystery forever. Best to do nothing under the circumstances.

"Charles was my brother," she said. "I know why he was killed."

An old woman scattered breadcrumbs for the pigeons. She shouldn't have been doing that. They breed diseases; they deface property; pigeons are a nuisance. Yes, there I was in the Central Park Zoo, a woman was giving me very important information. But I didn't know whether I was awake or whether I was asleep dreaming that I was in the Central Park Zoo. The dream seemed very real.

"Why are you telling me this? Wouldn't this be more appropriate information for the police?"

"I don't know that I can trust the police. And I don't think they'll investigate any more than they did already. They'll do as little as they can get away with and no more. It was just another hit and run as far as they're concerned."

"But you know otherwise."

"Larry Copland is responsible."

"I see why you didn't go to the police. What makes you think I'm easier to convince?"

"I know you want to find out who killed Sharon Hobart."

"Let me guess, the same people who killed your brother."

"It seems likely. She was mixed up with him. They were in business together, one might say."

"What business?"

"Selling corporate secrets."

As the story unfolded, it took on the hue of possibility. Lynn was Charles' half-sister. They had different mothers and had grown up in different households. They had lived near each other while children, Charles' mother reluctant to move away from the man she shared. Eventually, Lynn's mother got fed up with the sharing, but she didn't move away either. Her roots in the town, she wasn't going to be driven out. The children in the meantime struck up a clandestine friendship.

"I know Charles had a difficult side, but he was always good to me," Lynn said. "He wasn't as much of a monster as you may have heard or imagined."

"He was probably an eagle scout," I said.

"Charles and Sharon were high school sweethearts. The three of us were actually quite close; then we drifted apart. That was inevitable. Sharon's people and ours lived on opposite sides of the tracks. Our friendship was an anomaly. Of course, Sharon and Charles hooked up again later on.

"Charles confided his illegal activities to you?"

"No, he wouldn't involve me in any of that. He was very protective of me. I know he was in some kind of a mess the week he was killed. Charles was no stranger to trouble, but this time it was different. He looked more frazzled than I had ever seen him. It seemed as if he had gone in over his head. I didn't know the nature of the problem until he was dead. I found a diary that spelled out everything."

"It seemed odd to keep such a diary."

"Charles was very methodical when it came to business, and he thought of industrial espionage as just another business activity."

"You have this diary stashed away somewhere, no doubt."

"Yes, I'll be glad to show it to you if you'll help me."

"Help you do what?"

"Get Larry Copland. Even if Charles was stealing from Allied Chemicals, they had no right to kill him, did they?" Her voice faltered, as if she weren't quite sure.

"No," I said, "no right at all. Let's go take a look at this diary."

I had parked on 66th Street. I brought the conversation around to Sharon as we walked to the car.

"Sharon wasn't the easiest person for me to relate to all the time. She was using us you know, Charles and me, I mean. The friendship with us was her way of getting back at her father."

Lynn's apartment on the West Side was a walk-up in what had once been an elegant brownstone now broken up into apartments. She had concealed Charle's laptop on a closet shelf. Below, I couldn't help but notice a couple or furs that didn't come from a rummage sale. I looked around the room and made a quick calculation. Surprise, surprise, money came in here from somewhere. On the laptop, she opened a file that was supposed to be the diary. It seemed to have everything she had said: names, dates, places. It didn't prove anything against Larry or Allied Chemicals, but it certainly revealed a motive. Still, the material had to be authenticated.

"This information can be a hassle," I said. "Having it in your possession makes you a natural suspect. It implicates you in a way."

"It doesn't mention me at all."

"Did Charles subsidize your singing career?"

"No, not a penny."

"You're obviously not a pauper."

"I never said I was."

"You make a living from your music?"

"I wait on tables," she said seriously, as if she expected me to believe her.

"All of this from waiting on tables?"

"Big tips."

"I see."

She had been smart enough to make a couple of copies of the diary. I told her to find a safer place to hide it. She assured me she would. She handed me a disk with a copy. I left the apartment, but I never made it to my car.

As I emerged from the building, I felt a hulking presence approach from behind and push something metallic against my back. A black Toyota pulled up to the curb. Fortunately, one of those fortuitous events that are totally unremarkable unless they occur in conjunction with something else suddenly transpired. That is, a homeless person quite unexpectedly approached us. His bulbous nose had a crimson glow. "Would you gentlemen kindly spare some change?" he asked.

I rifled through my pockets and found nothing. "I'm all out of change Harry," I said to the man with the gun. "Do me a favor and give this gentleman something. I'll pay you back later."

"Beat it," Harry said to the down-and-out.

"Harry," I said in my most indignant voice. The vagabond seeing that he had an ally summoned his courage from wherever he had stored it and interposed himself between Harry and me. I bolted down the street. Harry pushed the beggar who, momentarily discarding passivity as he fell to the ground, grabbed Harry's legs causing Harry's upper part to make contact with the sidewalk.

Still in the car, Harry's accomplice no doubt assumed Harry could handle the street-person. The car man concentrated on me. He drove in pursuit thinking to cut me off at the corner. But I did him one better. I ducked into a service entrance. If these building were still anything like they were when I was a kid, the passageway would lead to the backyard. I could climb over the fence and exit through another building. They wouldn't know which building I was likely to pop out of; I might come out on the next block. If they wanted me they would have to follow.

I ran past a closed door behind which I heard a dog fiercely barking. A wave of primeval fear rippled through my body, but I reasoned that dogs can't leap through closed doors. At the back of the building there was a concrete barrier with a chain link fence on top. I would have to catapult myself up the wall, then the chain link fence. The dogs started barking again announcing that someone was close behind me.

"Hey you! What are you doing there?" an old woman shouted from a window.

"Telephone man," I shouted back.

"I'm calling the police," she screamed and disappeared from the window.

I hoped she was telling the truth, but I suspected it was an empty threat. Harry's partner was close behind me, but not so close that I couldn't lose him if I wanted to; but then, where would I be? Who were these guys? This was my chance to find out. On the other hand, they had at least one gun between them, probably two. Like a proper citizen, I was unarmed. However, fortune was with me. As I ducked into the arcade where the garbage cans were kept, I spotted a two-by-three just about the right length to make a dandy club. Harry's friend was in for a surprise, and who was to say that Harry wouldn't partake of it also? He had probably disentangled himself from the street-person and was on his way to assist his partner.

The gun worried me. I had to disable the guy before he had a chance to shoot. Luckily, since he thought I was running, I had surprise on my side. He would not predict my standing there waiting for him. If he were smart enough to foresee the ambush, he wouldn't be in the line of business he was in. The two-by-three over my shoulder like a bat, I flattened myself against the wall behind the garbage arcade.

I went for his knees. The wood on bone made a crunching sound. He collapsed like a folding box. I stood over him with the truncheon, and he instinctively brought up his arms to protect his face. I reached into his pocket to remove the gun. The shock of my sudden attack must have obliterated his awareness; otherwise I might have been a dead duck.

Terror sat on his face like a mask. His fear made me a bit uneasy. I had never thought of myself as someone who inspired terror. But I couldn't dwell on that right then. I had Harry to think about. He might prove harder to handle than his sidekick. To surprise Harry, I had to keep this guy quiet. I didn't quite know how to do that; a blow to the head might kill him. Of course, now I had his gun, but I doubted that was much of an advantage. A shoot-out was the last thing I wanted. After all, I wasn't Wyatt Earp.

Once the guy realized that I wasn't about to strike him again, he began to regain his courage.

"You're dead," he said, pain and anger distorting his face. "You're dead and you're crazy, but mostly you're dead."

"I like you too," I said.

"You're dead."

"You're a brilliant conversationalist," I said. "You'd go over big on a talk show."

Time was passing fast. To the right of me, there was a basement door—to the boiler room, no doubt. When I was a kid, the super of my building used to live in the basement apartment reached by going through a door like that one. I wondered whether supers still lived in such dismal spaces.

I tried the door, but it was locked. It didn't look like a very sturdy door. I went into it with my shoulder, but it didn't fly open the way doors did in movies. This wasn't my day. I could have shot the lock off, but that would make a lot of noise and alert Harry to my exact location. A pile of bricks rested under the external stairway that led up to the ground floor. I didn't bother to try that door; it would be locked for sure. I picked up a brick and slammed it against the lock. The tumbler fell apart. I pushed the door open. It led into a dark place.

"Get in there," I said to Harry's friend.

"Fuck you," he said. "I can't move. My fucken knees are broken."

I grabbed him by the collar and dragged him to the door. Pain kept him from resisting. I put the gun to his head, and I searched his pockets for a handkerchief. When I found it, I rolled it and gagged him. The whites of his eyes turned colors.

"Take off your jacket and your shirt," I said. He hesitated. I cocked the gun. He took off his jacket and his shirt. I put the gun in my belt while I ripped up the shirt and braided the strips together into a rope. I bound his hands with it; then I dragged him into the dark chamber. I left the door slightly ajar, so that I could see out. I didn't want to miss Harry when he came by. It seemed an interminable wait.

Finally, he appeared. He walked cautiously, not like his friend. He looked straight at the door, but he didn't come towards it. Gun in hand, he continued straight under the arcade towards the back of the building. When he had disappeared, I went out and picked up the two-by-three. I retrieved a tin can from the garbage and threw it across the yard. I flattened myself against the wall.

Harry doubled back to check out the noise. This curiosity

was his undoing. Alas, poor Harry, because he had the gun in his hand, I had to be rougher on him than I had been on his partner. The two-by-three came down on his gun hand first. The weapon dropped to the ground, and before he could dive for it, I wielded the two-by-three again, this time across his knees. I was starting to feel like a samurai master.

I dragged Harry over into the basement and tied him up with what was left of his partner's shirt. Now I had the two of them sitting there in semi-darkness. I searched around for a light switch, none. I walked a little further into the darkness. I found a pull chain. I pulled it, a forty watt bulb went on, not a lot of light but enough to see their faces as I questioned them.

"Okay guys," I said, "I want some answers."

Harry spat at me.

"I don't want to have to break any more bones," I said as I undid the gag on Harry's partner. "But I will, if I have to." I let that sink in.

It didn't sink in far enough. "Listen fellow, this is all a big mistake. We thought you were somebody else. So why don't we forget about the whole thing," Harry said.

"Shut up," I said. I searched them for ID. I took their wallets and cardholders.

"I didn't take you for a common thief," Harry said. "But if that's your bag..."

"Stuff it," I said.

All their ID's were in the cardholders, so I put their wallets back. Harry had about fifteen hundred dollars in his, but his name wasn't Harry. His driver's license had the name John Shultz. Harry suited him better. The other guy's name was Steve Conklin.

"So what's the story?" I asked casually. I was feeling lightheaded, as if I were standing outside myself watching someone else doing the interrogating.

"That's what we'd like to know," Harry said. (I couldn't help but think of him as Harry.)

"Why were you chasing me?"

"Because you have something that doesn't belong to you," Conklin said. He wasn't cool.

"I don't know what you're talking about," I confessed.

"It doesn't matter. You're a dead duck, a walking corpse. The minute you picked up that club you were dead."

That kind of talk began to unnerve me. "It seems to me you're in no position to make threats," I pointed out.

"That's right," Harry said. "But listen here, we're authorized to make a deal. You return our client's property, and we'll make it worth your while in cash."

"You're willing to pay for this diary?"

He smirked. "We don't want that trash."

"Well, that's all I have," I said.

"If you're lucky, you're lying."

"Just tell me what you want."

"This isn't getting us anywhere," Harry said.

"That's right, so let me tell you what I think is going on. Correct me if I'm wrong. Charles stole a valuable secret from Allied Chemicals, something easily concealable. Unable to bargain with him, or perhaps out of sheer vengeance, you killed him thinking that you knew how to retrieve the stolen information without him. But you were mistaken. More people were involved than you anticipated. There was Sharon. She had the information, or you thought she did. Being stupid, you didn't learn your lesson from having killed Charles. You killed Sharon when she refused to deal with you. So you were worse off than when you started. You killed off your best sources, and then you were groping in the dark. You decided that Sharon might have passed the information on to me, but this time you made a serious error. Not only do I not have the information, but also I'm not easy to kill. Moreover, I too am a vengeful person. I'm going to make you pay for Sharon's death. I can shoot you and claim self-defense. People saw you chasing me down the street, and these are your guns, after all, and even if the cops don't swallow that, no court will convict me. You know, crime of passion, crazed lover shoots murderers. You boys have reached the end of your road." I cocked one of the guns.

"You're fucking crazy," Conklin said.

"You have nothing to gain by shooting us," Shultz added.

"You're wrong," I assured him. "I have personal satisfaction to gain. And pretty boy here," I meant Conklin, "threatened me a couple of times. I don't want to have to worry about him coming after me. It makes sense to get rid of him now once and for all." That sounded convincing even to me.

"Charles died because he was stupid. His greed killed him," Conklin said.

"So you admit to killing him."

"I don't admit anything," he said. "What I'm saying is that we didn't ever get close enough even to talk to that woman. It doesn't look like it right now, but we're not as stupid as you think. She was our only link to the info our client is looking for, so as you said yourself, it wasn't in our interest to kill her. If anything, we were out to protect her."

"Well, judging from the outcome, it's plausible that those were your intentions, but being in the predicament that you're in, what else could you say?"

I pointed the gun at Conklin's head. Beads of perspiration sprouted all over his face. "Don't kill me," he said in a barely audible voice.

"We can prove that we didn't kill your friend," Shultz said.

I lowered the gun. "I'm listening."

"We took a picture of the killer."

"Hand it over."

"Don't be unreasonable. We don't carry it with us."

I raised the gun.

"That's the truth. We were following the Hobart woman, photographing her from afar, trying to get a clue that would lead us the stolen material. When she didn't appear on stage like she was supposed to, we looked for her. Eventually, we got to the roof just in time to snap the killer."

"Where is this photograph?"

"We'll take you to it."

"You tell me where it is. If it pans out, I'll send help."

"No way. We could be here for days. We could starve."

"You might come back and kill us anyway," Conklin said. He was convinced that I was crazed.

"I might do that if you're lying to me. I'm tired of talking to you guys. This is your last chance. Where can I get a hold of this photograph?"

"You can get it from Larry Copland," Shultz said.

"You're a clown," I said. "That doesn't do me any good. I can't go up to Larry Copland and say, 'You have the photograph of a killer; fork it over.'"

This information confirmed what I already suspected. Allied Chemicals was deeply involved in Sharon's murder. Larry was withholding evidence in a capital case. I might be able to get him on that, or at least make his life very uncomfortable for a while, if nothing else.

"That doesn't do me any good," I repeated, "and if it doesn't do me any good, it doesn't do you any either."

"Then you're going to have to kill us," Shultz said.

"I guess I'll have to," I said raising the gun. I backed up towards the door and cracked-up laughing. What tough guys! I could smell the fear. I went out and shut the door behind me. Before getting to the street, I unloaded the guns. I kept the bullets in my pocket but buried the pieces in the trash.

Chapter 20

I CALLED ROMANELLI and gave him a rundown of my adventure with Shultz and Conklin. I told him where he might find them, or rather, where I left them. I doubted that they would still be there. They weren't hurt enough to keep them from crawling out of that hole.

"I'll have them picked up," Romanelli said, "and the weapons, too. You should've held on to them." He wasn't going to miss a chance to needle me, as if we had been acquainted since childhood. "Bring the diary down here," he said.

"Sure, why not," I said. "How about tomorrow morning? I need to shower and change. I don't smell so good."

"I'm not asking you to a formal ball. Come down right now," he said. "Who knows what tomorrow might bring?"

"That kind of talk is not reassuring," I said.

"It's not meant to be," he answered. "If security is what you wanted, you should've stayed out of this. But it's too late now, isn't it? Come down. You'll be safe in the station house." He was enjoying thinking of me in a mess.

"You're a real pal," I said. "I'll be right down."

When I got to Romanelli's door, he was sitting at his desk—the metal job. He got up and extended his hand—a firm grip.

"Sit down," he said.

I sat down in the vinyl-covered armchair.

"Would you like some coffee?" He was being real nice.

"Sure," I said. He fetched two cups of coffee from a coffee machine at the other end of the floor. When he had settled himself back in his seat, he said, "Now, run this whole thing by me again."

I proceeded to tell him as much of the story as I thought he needed to know. He sat there swinging back in his swivel chair and stroking his chin with his thumb and index finger. He was trying to give the impression of thoughtfulness, but it was a quality foreign to him, like a coat three sizes too large.

"Well, it all sounds very interesting," he said, when I had finished, "but it isn't much to build a case on. You know that, don't you?"

"It all points in the right direction," I said.

"Does it? Consider this: we haven't got a case against Copland unless his own thugs testify against him, and what do you think the chances of that are? A snowball in hell would get better odds. Those pigeons flew the coop by now. If they're smart, they're not going to let themselves be found. So what do we do? Go up to Copland and say, 'We know you ordered a hit on Charles Osgood and Sharon Hobart, so confess'?"

"Let's say for a minute that Shultz was telling the truth about having photographed the killer, then Copland is withholding evidence."

"Another killer, we got too many killers in this case. We got Macully left to right, and that's all we really need. Then we got Shultz and Conklin for good measure, in case we need a couple understudies, and now you say there is another one. What are we going to do with all these killers? Enough is enough."

"Maybe Shultz and Conklin didn't photograph any killer; maybe they just told me that story; maybe they're the killers, but if they are, then Copland is our man. They work for him."

"Pure speculation."

"So where do we go from here?"

"If we find Conklin and Shultz, we'll try to get a search warrant for Copland's office and home. Maybe we'll turn up something, maybe not. It may take a few days to get a warrant, if we can get one. There's no judge who's going to be happy swearing out a warrant on a prominent citizen."

"We have to find a way to rattle him," I said.

"Yeah, Shultz and Conklin are the key," after a pause he added, "You could've blown them away and got your revenge. That would've been the simple way."

"I want to get Copland," I said. The virulence in my own voice surprised me a little.

"She meant that much to you?"

I didn't answer.

"I'm sorry," he said.

"So let's grab Copland."

"Nothing we can do there unless we get a lucky break."

"Like what?"

"Like he cracks and confesses."

We weren't going to be that lucky, but we did get a break of sorts.

Chapter 21

MY PHONE RANG, and when I put it up to my ear, a stranger's voice started out with a question.

"Mr. Navarro?"

"For sure."

"Hold on Mr. Navarro, Mr. Copland will speak to you."

I hadn't asked to speak to Mr. Copland, unless I was losing my memory.

"Hello Navarro, how are you?"

"Surprised, and very well," I said.

"It's time we have a talk. Two intelligent men should be able to work out minor differences without resorting to sordid methods. Don't you think?"

"Talk, I'm listening."

"Not like this," he said. "Come to my office."

I didn't like that, but I went. I took a taxi up to Columbus Circle. The Allied Chemicals headquarters was just north of the circle overlooking Central Park. At the desk in the lobby, I was confronted by security. I expected a whole hassle explaining who I was and whom I had come to see, but as soon as the guard heard my name he said, "All ready for you," and he handed me a security pass and instructed me to take the express elevator to the top floor. When I got there, a svelte young woman greeted me and led me to Copland's door.

Larry Copland's office was exactly what I expected—about the size of a basketball court. Behind his desk, the window made up the whole wall providing a panoramic view as if the whole city had been put there for his personal convenience. As I walked across the room toward his desk, the disadvantage of being on his ground became immediately obvious. He pretended to be intent on some papers in front of him, and he didn't get up until I was a few steps from his desk. Suddenly, he shed all semblance of being a busy man. As if we were at the country club, he exuded complete ease.

A sitting area occupied one side of the room, a chesterfield, apposite a leather chair, and a coffee table in-between. "Let's sit over here. It'll be more comfortable," he said. He sat in the chair. I sat across from him.

"Drink?" he asked.

"No thanks," I said. I didn't want to get too chummy. I had the distinct sense that I was being set up for something.

"You're an interesting fellow," he said. "There's no reason why there should be any enmity between us."

"Is there any?"

"You're investigating a murder."

"That's right."

"My people tell me that in the course of your investigation you've come across certain information that belongs to this company. That was, shall we say, unlawfully removed."

"And what information is that?"

"A certain chemical formula that we've been developing for some time. It can put Allied Chemicals far ahead of its competitors. Of course, nobody can steal our proprietary right. We can prove that we've been developing this idea for years. But we have to introduce the product while they still have no inkling of what our actual tack has been. They'll develop something similar right at our heels, but this little time edge, which might seem like nothing to you, means billions of dollars to this company. You can appreciate this I'm sure. I know you're an astute businessman. I see no reason why we shouldn't be able to do business. I know you're not adverse to making money."

I sat there thinking over what he was saying. Did he really

know so little about me? I had assumed he was smarter than that. On the other hand, he might just be playing a game. Maybe he was only trying to make me think he was dense. His perfectly tailored suit, his manicured finger nails, his hair cut, which seemed as if every hair had been individually cut and set in place, told me he was a man who didn't overlook details.

"I always made money on the up and up. I don't need to sell industrial secrets."

"I'm quite sure of that," he said. "Don't get me wrong. I'm not suggesting that you were in any way intentionally involved in this sordid little scheme. No, by no means, I know you're a man of impeccable integrity. I'm not offering you this deal because I think you're out to make a fast buck, no, no. Consider it a small reward, a finder's fee, a token of the company's appreciation. I know you have been greatly inconvenienced, to say the least, by the turn of events."

Greatly inconvenienced! I was ready to throttle him. But it was an inconvenient place to do it, his own office. No doubt he had security guards standing right outside the door, but I could bide my time.

"I had a friend murdered. You call that an inconvenience?"

"I call that a misfortune."

"And you expect me to forget about it and let you get away with it?"

"Get away with it? Dear Marco, you don't mind if I call you Marco, I had absolutely nothing to do with the tragic end of your lady friend. You must see that. After all, isn't your having a lady friend other than Frannie to my advantage?"

The more he spoke, the slimier he seemed. I pictured him sliding and coiling over his leather couch.

"You had Charles killed, but he didn't have the formula on him; you assumed Sharon had it, so you went after her, isn't that so? And now you're trying to buy me off."

"Come, be reasonable; consider the facts. Your friend's murder was not a professional job. I don't have people murdered, but if I did, I would certainly deal only with professionals. That stands to reason, don't you think?"

Of course it did, and I had already thought of that angle, but that was only a hypothesis. In reality, things tend to get out of hand. The killer might have decided to add a little spice to life.

"I had nothing to do with that young lady's death." He leaned forward toward me as if to impart a secret, "I can prove it."

"Well?" I queried looking straight into his passionless blue eyes.

"You have something I want, and I have something that seems of interest to you. Perhaps we can work out an exchange."

"You mean you're willing to sell out one of your henchmen."

"You do have a melodramatic turn of mind. I assure you that you will be satisfied that I am entirely in the clear. In any case, you have nothing to lose."

"Okay, lay it on me." I thought he was bluffing, and I was ready to call him on it. But he wasn't going to play my way.

"I'm not sure you're holding any cards," he said smiling as if he were having a grand time. "So it would be foolish of me to put everything on the table right now. Suffice it to say that my people kept a close watch on Charles and his acquaintances in an effort to retrieve the stolen property. They might have come across something that might be of use to you. They might have even taken photographs of people you might want to interview."

That was clear enough. He had something to trade, a

photograph of the killer. Of course, I didn't have what he was looking for, or at least I didn't think I did.

"This formula means so much to you that you would withhold evidence in a criminal investigation? A woman was murdered; doesn't that mean anything to you?"

"I assure you, I'm not the monster you're making me out to be." He leaned back quite relaxed. His eyes brightened. "Your friend is dead and that's regrettable, but I still have to run this company. Powerful and invulnerable as I may seem from where you sit, if this company falters, there will be wolves at my throat. That formula has to keep them at bay a while longer, until I come up with something else to fend them off. I have to use every means at my disposal even if it means being rather ungenerous to you. I have valuable information. It may be valuable to others besides you. If you don't come up with the formula, I have to continue dealing. I hope you understand my position."

Perhaps I had painted myself into a corner. I had to come up with the goods, but I didn't have them. Copland too was beginning to think that I didn't have them. I had to stall for time. "This formula is no longer just something that was stolen from you. Now it's evidence in two murders. It should go to the police."

"That would be risky for me. The police aren't good at keeping secrets. And it would gain you nothing."

"Maybe not," I said getting up.

"Don't be hasty," he said. "I'll be seeing you at the Thompsons' on Friday, I hope." He was referring to a dinner party at Bella's.

"Yes," I said, "God willing." It was the sort of thing I never said, but I couldn't help saying it at that moment.

When I got home I pored over Charles' diary trying to find a clue as to where that formula might be, but no luck.

The answer wasn't in the diary. If it was, I didn't see it. Let's say Charles had it with him the night he was killed, and suppose he passed it to Sharon on the dance floor. She must have brought it up to my place. Why would she have left it here as Copland thought? She knew they would search my place. They did and didn't find anything. So what did she do with it? My pondering began to give me a headache, and I wasn't getting anywhere going over the same things over and over.

The phone rang. It was Frannie. She was calling from the street. Could she come up? Sure, why not? I needed a break anyway. She entered in her usual sprightly manner. She threw her jacket on the first convenient piece of furniture and sat down, or rather, she slinked forward, one elbow on the arm of the couch, her hand propping up her chin. She had an impish grin on her face.

"You don't look well," she said.

"Thanks."

"Don't be upset. I don't think it's a permanent condition."

"I have a problem," I said.

The corner of her eyes wrinkled up in an amused squint, as if to say that she had been waiting a long time for this moment.

"What's your problem?"

"It has to do with your hubby to be," I said. "Do you really want to hear about it?"

"Oh no, not you too. Everybody is down on me about him. I expected a little support from you. You're supposed to be my friend."

"Okay, I'll say no more about it. That's the best I can do under the circumstances. You don't expect me to be happy about your marrying another guy."

"Don't be like that Marc. I have to marry somebody, and I can't marry you. Don't look at me that way. You know it

199

wouldn't work out. I would make you very unhappy. You know how difficult I am."

"Enough said on this subject, okay?"

"Okay, with me. Let's talk about something else."

"Help me with this," I said. "Sharon had a piece of information that she might have hidden in this apartment, or maybe somewhere else. But if you were her and you had some object with information on it, where would you hide it?"

"If I were her, I would destroy it."

"No, then it would be gone, and all the effort to get it would have been wasted."

"Not in Sharon's case," Frannie looked rather triumphant at that moment. She knew something. "I guess it's all right to tell. Now that she's dead, she won't care." She paused to consider whether that was really true. "Sharon had a photographic memory. She could memorize anything and have perfect recall."

"I see, but why was that a secret?"

"She didn't want to be considered a freak. Very few people knew, and those who did were sworn to secrecy."

"So if anyone wanted to suppress information that had been passed to her, they would most likely have to kill her to do so."

"Yes, crude and simple but effective."

The circumstances still pointed toward Copland as the culprit. Believe it or not, for Frannie's sake, I was hoping that he had told me the truth about not being involved in Sharon's death. She seemed hell bent on that marriage. I didn't want to spoil it for her, or so I told myself. Still, Copland had a motive and the machinery in place to carry out an execution.

"Did you ever tell anybody else about Sharon's photographic memory?"

"Of course not. She didn't want me to."

"Not even Larry?"

"No one," she insisted.

He could have found out some other way. But why then was he going through the charade with me about finding the formula? To make sure that she indeed had destroyed the physical copy? Of course! He was very thorough. If there was a copy, he knew I would find it to trade for the killer. I could call his bluff and see whom he would come up with to take the rap. Then I would have something to work with. The fall guy might not like being in that position. He might squeal.

"Larry might turn out to be all right," I said to Frannie.

"Yes, of course, he's all right."

"He might have a line on the killer."

"You see? He'll cooperate with you. He's like the rest of us. He wants to be liked."

She was in for a rude awakening. But I gave up trying to warn her. "He's bringing me some evidence on Friday, when we meet at your mother's."

Chapter 22

WHEN I ARRIVED at the Thompson's on Friday night, a body was being wheeled out to a waiting ambulance. As usual, a crowd of onlookers obstructed the sidewalk. I figured some poor slob had a heart attack. I resolved to renew my membership at the health club, but before I stopped musing about my health, I spied the lieutenant looking rather dour as he followed the stretcher. A uniform tried to impede my progress.

"It's all right," Romanelli said to the patrolman, "let him pass."

From Romanelli's facial expression, I could have sworn he had a mouth full of ashes. I excluded heart attack as the cause of death.

"Your theory is down the toilet," Romanelli said. "That's Copland stretched out there."

"Yeah?" I said. Not very eloquent, but I was thinking of Frannie not being in very good shape at the moment.

"Did he have any photographs on him?" I asked.

Romanelli gave me an inquisitive look. "No," he said, "not even in his wallet."

"What happened?"

"Don't know for sure. He splattered on the courtyard. He wasn't the type to commit suicide, so I'd say he was pushed. No sign of a struggle though."

"How long ago?"

"Not long, about half an hour."

"Come with me. I have a hunch. You better seal the building. The killer is still in there."

"Come off it. We're not amateurs here. Nobody is getting out of this building without my knowledge. Don't antagonize me Navarro. You need me."

He followed me into the elevator, and we rode up.

"For Christ sake, are you going to keep me in the dark forever? Don't forget I'm the investigator on this case. You're just a civilian withholding evidence."

"Quite so, quite so," I said.

"Copland told me he had evidence, photographs of the killer. He was bringing them to me."

"He was killed for the pictures. The killer knew he was bringing them. Who did you tell?" There was no conviction in his voice. He was playing with me.

"Only one person."

"That's our man."

"I told Frannie."

"Our woman then."

"Don't be ridiculous, Frannie wouldn't have killed Copland, especially by throwing him from a high place."

"She knocked him unconscious first, dragged him to the window and shoved him out."

"But why? She didn't kill Sharon."

"That's only a slight technicality. We can iron it out later."

"This line of work has really poisoned your sense of humor."

"You think so? So who killed Copland?"

We reached the twenty-first floor.

"You'll know when we find the pictures."

Bella answered the door.

"Marc," she said, "I'm so glad you're here. Frannie is in such a state. I don't know what to do. She'll feel better when she sees you."

We followed her down the hallway. In the living room

Frannie was sitting in one corner of the couch, her knees tucked-up to her chin. She had been crying, but she didn't look as bad as I expected. She managed a feeble smile when she looked up at me. It occurred to me that she might be enjoying playing the role of the bereaved girlfriend.

"I'm afraid somebody we know killed Larry," I said.

"Marc, how can you say that? None of us associate with that sort of people," Bella said. Knowing full well that she had no idea what kind of people her children associated with when out of her sight, she looked around questioningly. Frannie's falling for Larry Copland had been a complete surprise to her. Still, even if he wasn't an ideal suitor, he wasn't the sort to fling his own body off a roof. Paul was a different story. The lowlifes didn't repel him. She suspected that they might even attract him. He was an unpredictable boy, but she had faith that all the years she had spent nurturing him had done some good.

"Larry knew who killed Sharon, and he was bringing evidence. He was killed to prevent that."

"How does it follow that it was somebody we know?"

"I only told one person that Larry was bringing something for me."

"And that was Frannie," Romanelli said.

"You're not suggesting Frannie killed anybody!" Bella exclaimed. "That's preposterous!"

"I'm not saying she did it," Romanelli continued. "All I'm saying is that she knows who did."

"This is ridiculous," Frannie said. "I didn't discuss Larry's coming here with anybody, much less any evidence."

"With nobody at all?" Romanelli queried.

"Nobody outside this family."

"So there we go. That narrows it down considerably."

"Marc, don't just stand there. Say something. You don't think one of my children is a killer, do you?"

I didn't know what to say. I didn't want to be in that position. Part of my life was slipping away from me. I was about to lose the Thompsons forever. "I'm not making any judgments, Bella. I'm just trying to follow the evidence."

"So you discussed it with your brother?" Romanelli continued.

"No, I didn't," Frannie blurted. "How can I remember everything? I'm not up to this right now. Please leave me alone."

"Marc, how can you do this to us?"

"He's not doing anything ma'am. I'm in charge of this investigation," Romanelli said. "You knew Copland was bringing evidence," he continued turning to Paul.

"I didn't know anything of the sort," Paul retorted.

"This doesn't make any sense at all," Frannie interjected. "What makes you think nobody else knew about this supposed evidence?"

"What indeed?" A voice broke into the conversation. "The door was open, so I took the liberty," Lynn Fromowitz said as she stood at the door of the living room.

Frannie seemed to be the only one not surprised by her appearance. "I guess you heard about Larry," Frannie said trying to keep the tears from welling up.

"I did," Lynn simply stated. Her voice had a flinty quality I hadn't noticed before.

"Who are you, and what are you doing here?" Romanelli asked the sensible questions.

"I'm Lynn Fromowitz," she said. Larry Copland asked me to bring a small package to him here." She took a small manila envelope from her purse, flashed it at us, then dropped it back into her purse.

"Hand over the envelope," Romanelli said in his most New York cop voice.

She reached into the purse again, but this time she brought out a stubby little pistol.

"I'll give you five seconds to put that away," Romanelli said.

"Shut up!" she barked, but the brashness embarrassed her. "Larry was going to make a trade," she said modulating to a more ladylike tone. "So let's make a trade. I have the picture, so give me the formula."

"What the hell are you talking about?" Romanelli asked.

"Okay, I have the envelope right here," I said delving into my breast pocket.

Groping for the manila envelope, she reached into the purse again.

"No, you promised," Paul shrieked as he lunged at Lynn.

The gunshot sounded unreal, a sound totally inappropriate to the surroundings. The body didn't stagger backward from the force of the bullet but rather crumbled to the floor much like a deflating balloon. For an instant, nobody moved. Lynn seemed more surprised than anyone that the gun had gone off. She didn't move as Romanelli removed the weapon from her hand. The other two women sprang to Paul's side. Romanelli called for the medics, but it was useless. The shot was fatal.

Chapter 23

SOMETIMES I DREAMT about Frannie and sometimes about Sharon, and sometimes in my dreams the one who looked like Sharon was called Frannie, and the one who looked like Frannie was called Sharon. But when I woke up, neither one of them was there. No matter who else was in bed with me, those two were also there, and that made for a very crowded bed and a very empty life.

I decided to pay my mother a visit, so I headed down to the sunshine state, the geriatric playground. I took a taxi out to the airport, and all the while I felt like a runaway, or rather like an escaped convict. Any minute I expected the taxi driver to turn around and reveal his true identity as an agent who would demand to see my traveling papers. In such an eventuality, I imagined, I would fumble through my pockets in a futile attempt to find the non-existent permits, not once resorting to the incontrovertible argument that "This is America, buddy. We don't operate that way here."

I sat in the back seat of the cab getting lost in its spaciousness. It wasn't difficult. Perhaps in the vastness of this backseat he wouldn't find me, even if he were indeed a trained agent trying to prevent my escape. I looked at the passing scenery, and it was gray and very ordinary. Nothing at all, except the names of places indicated where we were. It could have been in any number of cities in America or Europe, or the rest of the world for that matter. I, however, wasn't going through any of those places at the moment. Attempting to escape my own imagination, I traveled through an imaginary landscape. I had a strong suspicion that I couldn't exit such a place via taxi, but I knew no other method, and I was willing at the moment to try the obvious despite the apparent futility.

The airport seemed fraught with dangers. It wasn't the friendly place it had once been in my adolescence when I went there with friends to stare at the gateway to adventure, much like boys of another century who had gone down to the docks to gaze at the tall ships. But now there were glass partitions everywhere, bulletproof no doubt, and checkpoints with metal detectors and x-ray machines for the luggage, somewhere out of sight perhaps even the dogs that sniff out explosives. All of these precautions made me suspicious of all fellow travelers. I looked out for crooked noses and shifty eyes, for telltale scars and tattoos.

The taxi driver turned out to be a benign fellow, graciously accepted a tip when proffered—he didn't smirk knowingly, his vacuous face spoke only of simple pastimes, beer drinking and betting on the horses. The porter, likewise harmless, carried the luggage to its proper place without revealing any covert motive or occupation. Perhaps their craft was too much for me to discern, but I discounted that possibility.

I found myself boarding the plane. The flight attendant by the door smiled cheerfully as she reached out for my ticket. My relief was palpable; I had maneuvered through the obstacles and had but a short way to go before I sank into the lap of an airline seat. Once in the clouds my mind was much eased. I had affected an escape of sorts, and my view through the window confirmed it. The amorphous world of clouds and sky was the very thing I needed.

My mother was much the same as when I had last seen her. She had settled into a plateau of arrested age, a warp where time did not exist. I needed that fantasy. She still loved the beach; she had always. I was still indifferent to it. The Florida sun was too bright. It made every object unrealistically sharp. The sand was yellow and water was blue and beyond that the sky was also blue. My mother wore a straw hat and a red cover-up. We went down to the beach because it was her routine, and there was no reason to alter it for me. She talked about her everyday life and what was going on with this or that friend, but the words came to me muffled as if I were holding a conch shell to my ear.

"And you?" she asked. "You're unusually silent."

She was right, but it was not my fault. I was full of words. They formed in my mind but died before reaching my mouth. They fell like lead to the bottom of my self. I was filling up with dead words. Would they putrefy? I wondered.

"Talk to me," she said, her voice unusually deep.

"There was this woman," I started, and I told her the story as best I could, somewhat incoherently.

"Ah, well, there's more than one woman in this story," she remarked. "The dead one you have to let go, or she'll ruin your life just as surely as the other one will if you let her." She said that with great conviction.

"Did a ghost ruin your life?" I asked. She remained silent, so that I was sorry I had asked the question, not so much for her sake as for mine. I was afraid to hear the answer.

"No," she finally said, "I had you to save me." She smiled as she said that, but her eyes were far away.

"You must have been lonely," I said.

"No, I was too busy."

"But at night, while I slept, it must have been difficult."

"I had a good life," she affirmed. "It was hard, of course, after your father was gone, but I adjusted. You will too. And for you, at least, the choices are simpler."

"I suppose so," I said though really nothing seemed simple at the moment. Who was there to save me? "Only yourself," she would have said, had I asked, but I didn't.

"Tell me," she said, "How did you know Paul was the killer?"

"I didn't," I said. "All my actions at that point were totally intuitive, like sleep walking, and when I woke up, I was in a total muddle."

That was the only explanation I could come up with, and yet it made no sense at all. Romanelli had asked me the same question, and I gave him the same answer, though with him it had not been easy. It was embarrassing not to be able to be more rational when talking to another man. His initial reaction was what I had feared it would be, disbelief closely followed by derision, but he caught himself—he couldn't argue with the result. Then he came full circle. "Maybe you're a natural," he said. "Maybe you have a special ability to smell out perpetrators. Have you ever considered joining the police force?" The thought was so bizarre that I was struck dumb. He put the best interpretation on my silence taking it for serious thought and sparing me the chagrin of having offended him.

As always, his praise was alloyed. He quickly followed with, "Of course, Fromowitz completely bamboozled you. You had no inkling of what she was up to, did you?"

I hemmed and hawed for a minute, but he was basically right. I hadn't paid attention to the obvious signs of something amiss. I saw them all right, but I chose to ignore them. Our first meeting couldn't have been accidental, but I didn't see anything strange in her attention to me. Chalk that one up to vanity. But then, when I had seen her apartment, why didn't I pursue my initial hunch that she was not altogether what she pretended to be?

"Well that's all right," Romanelli said. "You're not trained to think that way."

"You mean I could be?"

"Of course," he said.

He was serious. It dawn on me that he was paying me the highest compliment at his disposal. I had grown to like him too.

Alongside my mother on the beach, I had to deal with something else.

"You haven't woken up yet," she said.

"You mean this might all be a bad dream."

"It will seem so before long."

"I hope so," I said half to myself, and I closed my eyes and turned my head up to the sun, hoping that it might burn away the fog that seemed to have settled stubbornly over me.

"You know, nothing good could have come out of your involvement with Sharon Hobart. So on that score, you're not altogether in the red," she said mixing some metaphors but getting her meaning across nevertheless.

I understood her morality. It was the same as in some Hollywood movies. An adulterous woman had to come to a bad end.

"This Frannie is not my cup of tea either, but maybe she's what you need."

Surprised, I looked up at her. This was the first encouraging thing she had said about any woman since my marriage to Gail. "You think I need more hassle in my life."

"Well, you're the one who put it that way. A good sign, you're beginning to see her the way she really is."

"Ma, I never said she was easy."

"Only exciting."

"Yes," I conceded begrudgingly.

"That's enough at the beginning," she said, "but not for long."

"Well, it doesn't matter, does it? She's gone."

"I wouldn't bet on it," she said.

She must have had her usual wry smile on her calm face,

but I didn't see it. My gaze was fixed on a slim familiar figure, in a black and yellow swimsuit, approaching from the direction of the sea.